The Valerons - Winter Kill

The cold and blizzards of the winter of 1886–87 changed the way of life in cattle country forever. But, while winter storms might bring many things in the world to a standstill, evil never rests, and romance doesn't follow a season or timetable.

Jared Valeron had become embroiled in the search for a killer, but ends up taking a load of freight to aid Nash Valeron and the people of Castle Point. As fate would have it, the small town is also a refuge for a pack of outlaws. Having committed a brazen double robbery that left several soldiers dead, the leaders of the combined criminal gangs do not get along. Their shaky alliance is further challenged by the severe weather preventing them from travel.

Jared learns the miscreant band intends to ransack the town when they leave. Knowing the outlaws are killers, Jared recruits a teamster and a couple of townsmen to help him do the impossible: put twelve men in custody, in a town with few able men, and no sheriff or jail. If his plan fails, it could mean death and ruination for the entire town… including his brother and his wife.

The Valerons - Winter Kill

Terrell L. Bowers

A Black Horse Western

ROBERT HALE

ISBN 978-0-7198-3142-3

The Crowood Press
The Stable Block
Crowood Lane
Ramsbury
Marlborough
Wiltshire SN8 2HR

www.bhwesterns.com

Robert Hale is an imprint
of The Crowood Press

*For my beloved son-in-law, Brook Williams, who was taken
much too soon, but left us with many fond memories.*

CHAPTER ONE

The raiders arrived in the middle of the night, with faces covered, carrying torches and brandishing guns. Grant Roderick, who had been ill for some time, managed, with the use of his crutches, to move out to the porch and confront them. He had no weapon, but his son arrived and stood by his side with a shotgun, ready to blast away if the visit turned violent.

'This is your last warning, Roderick!' A hooded man spoke up. 'One week from today, we'll use these torches and turn this place to ashes. Come morning, we're going to push a thousand head of cattle towards your north meadows. Any of those red and white mongrel beef we see will be shot where they stand. The McMasters name is going to be the only brand in this part of Montana.'

'We've been here for almost ten years,' Grant growled a reply. 'What gives you bunch of interlopers the right to come on to my land and give me orders?'

'The guns we are holding, along with these torches, Roderick,' the masked man threatened. 'We don't want bloodshed, but we are taking over this valley. It's your choice – take your cattle and git, or stick around and be buried here.'

Roderick choked back the inferno of rage that flooded his very being. His first impulse was to jump off the porch, yank the speaker from the back of his horse and pound him into the dust. However, he barely had the strength in his ailing body to remain standing upright.

'Now, see here…' he began, but his prolonged illness had left him weak and impotent. The retort died on his lips, the sudden tightness in his chest and a tingling down his left arm removing any notion of fighting back. He swallowed his pride and watched in silence as the bunch of riders turned their animals and raced off into the night.

'What do you want to do, Pa?' Christopher asked, having not offered a word during the exchange. 'We can't hope to win a fight against McMasters and his bunch of hired gunmen. And the army has made it clear they won't intervene in free grazing land disputes. With no real law in Montana, we're on our own.'

'I know, son. I know.'

'Thomson and Coogan pulled out yesterday. The others are sticking with us, but none of them wants to get into a range war we can't win. As it stands, we've barely enough men for a cattle drive.'

Grant heaved a sigh. 'Do you remember our conversation after we made that sale in Chicago last year?'

'Yeah, back when we attended the big cattle auction.'

'We don't have a choice now, son. Come daylight, have the men get their belongings in order, then start rounding up the herd. Soon as we're able, we'll point them south and won't look back.'

'You intend we should go all the way to the Colorado border? That's a long, difficult drive. With only the few of us left to manage four hundred head of cattle, we might not make it at all.'

6

'Hire a couple more drovers,' he directed. 'Use what money we have left. Promise our boys and any new hires top dollar when we reach Wyoming.' After a moment's hesitation, he added: 'Offer a second bonus if we lose fewer than fifty head.'

'Once I have the boys rounding up the beef, I'll ride over to Helena. I can probably hire four or five more men. That ought to be enough. Meanwhile, Cookie can get the chuck wagon ready to go.' Chris paused, giving his father a grim look. 'You and Cookie are not in the best of shape for a six- to eight-week trail drive.'

'Just do as I say, son,' Grant said quietly. 'I'll ride with the chuck wagon, but we both know I won't make it as far as Wyoming. The main thing, McMasters isn't going to get the best of us. We're giving up this house and our ranch, but we won't let his greed wipe out the herd we've built.' In a rare show of affection, he placed his hand on Christopher's shoulder. 'This is your legacy now, and I couldn't be more proud of you. Just remain the kind of man I've known and respected all these years.'

'I won't let you down, Pa. That's a promise.'

***

Jared Valeron, in an effort to avoid another dry, dusty, tedious trail drive, had accompanied Faro to the town of Rimrock. The Valerons supplied coal to the feed, storage and coal company there, and it was time to renew their contract. Faro was in charge of the Valeron coal mine and met with the owner. The bickering on price and the tonnage needed was about as much fun as fishing in a dry lake bed.

Rather than sit in on the boring negotiating and haggling, Jared spent the time wandering around town. He had been there a few times and knew a couple of people. He was pleasantly surprised when he spotted a deputy US marshal he recognized sitting in the café having a meal. As the fellow was alone, Jared entered the dining room and walked over to join him. He ordered a cup of coffee and sat down at the table.

'I'll be switched!' Jared greeted him. 'JR, what are you doing in Wyoming? I thought you were strictly a Colorado and New Mexico lawman.'

John Reinhold was about thirty, with a ready smile and thinning hair. He was a fairly large man, well over six feet tall, and looked as if he could have been built by railroad ties. His paw engulfed Jared's hand as he reached over to shake hands.

'What do you say, Valeron?' he returned the query. 'You must be lost, too!'

Jared explained what he was doing in Rimrock, then asked the deputy his business.

'Been chasing dust in a wind storm, Valeron,' he admitted gravely. 'Got us one of them repeat killers. You know the kind I mean – he's done been going all over the country and kilt several gals what work in saloons or parlours. First one we learnt about was over in Leadville, then a second was found in Denver. A third victim turned up at Junction City about a month ago. Last week, it was right here in Rimrock.'

'Sounds like a travelling man… maybe a drummer or salesman of some kind.'

'Been talking to everyone in town and got nothing,' the deputy said in disgust. 'Same with all four murders, no one has seen a blessed thing.'

'Could be, the culprit is riding the rails. Other than this town, the other places you mentioned are pretty much along the mainline tracks.'

'We done checked with conductors at every station, compared tickets of travellers getting on and off – and got no matches at all. I suppose the guy could change his name for every trip, or he maybe jumps on the train and sneaks into each station, but the railroad has people watching for that. I figure he'd have been spotted at least once.'

'What about the saloons and gentleman parlours?' Jared asked. 'You telling me no one has seen a suspicious sort with any of the four victims?'

'Man's a ghost.' He grimaced his disgust. 'And there's nothing gentlemanly about this killer. Each of them poor souls were strangled and buried in the trash behind or near their places of business.'

'Sounds like an utterly vicious killer.'

'Yeah. The only clue – if you can call it a clue – is that he takes a hank of hair from each of his victims. I reckon it could be a morbid souvenir or the like. I ask you, Valeron, is that 'bout as crazy as snortin' loco weed, or what?'

'Never heard of such a thing, JR,' Jared mused woefully. 'Who would want to kill harmless doves of the evening?'

'He's got us stumped, wandering blind and totally clueless. And that's the truth.'

'How about employees from the train? Anyone check on them?'

'Not one railroad employee was at all of three regular stops, and no trace of any of them here in Rimrock. Plus it's quite a ways from here to the nearest railway station.'

'So you've got absolutely nothing to work with,' Jared concluded. 'No witnesses, no trail to follow, no idea where to look next.'

'There's too many drifters, salesmen, tramps, stage-coach passengers or freighters – the list of suspects is every man who wanders through any one of those places where a killing took place.'

Jared sighed. 'Like wearing a blindfold and trying to hit a jack rabbit with a rock. Not much chance of success.'

JR bobbed his head. 'Would you be lookin' to toss your badge in on this? Brett was durn good at running down a killer, but he's a family man now. Still, I remember how he used to brag that you were the best tracker in the entire country. What do you say?'

'I'm only a once-in-a-while deputy,' Jared told him. 'And your superiors don't hold with some of my tactics. Brett has saved me from being locked away for more than one of the jobs I took for the marshal's office.'

The deputy grinned. 'You mean like hanging three kidnappers without giving them a trial? Brett told me about that one.'

'It was our sister,' Jared defended his actions. 'And those stinkin' kidnappers killed the man she was going to marry... a day before the wedding.'

JR held up both hands, palms outward. 'Hey! You don't have to justify your actions with me. Don't know if Brett ever told you, but I arrested a guy who had abused a little kid a coupla years back. The high-ups were not happy that I brought him in with two broken arms. They didn't believe he had put up that much of a fight.'

'I remember Brett mentioning it. He said the pervert was barely five feet tall and built like a scarecrow. I can see the higher echelons'... what's the word? scepticism?'

The deputy laughed. 'I admit my temper got the best of me. But, damn, anyone who would hurt a little girl...' and with an accusatory gaze at Jared: 'You'd have killed him, for sure.'

'Hanged him high from the nearest tree,' Jared didn't argue his conclusion.

'You doing anything important?' Reinhold got back to business. 'We could sure use the help.' At Jared's hesitation, the deputy went forward. 'I'll let the marshal's office know you are going to check the route to the south and east. I'm supposed to continue west, after I check out Laramie.'

'I suppose I could ride through a few stops between here and Deliverance, then maybe Junction City and Denver, in case the murdering snake is making a circle that direction. I was going to visit my brother in Castle Point, and maybe slip over and see one of my cousins in Deliverance. Don't expect either of them to make it home for any of the family holidays.'

'Let me pay for the meal. I'll take you over to my hotel room and you can take a look at all of the information we've collected. It might give you a little more background for the hunt.'

Jared sighed, 'I probably should have let Faro come to his meeting in Rimrock alone. I've a feeling it's going to be a long, cold winter, chasing after an unknown, murdering slug.'

***

Reese walked into the main Valeron home and marched over to Locke Valeron's desk. He tossed the invoice down on top of the journal the man had been working on.

'We took a major beating on the sale of this last herd of cattle,' he complained to his father. 'Barely paid us for the trouble to ship them back east.'

'Prices have been in a dive for the past two or three years,' Locke said, not hiding his dejection. 'Too many cattle on the range these days. We've got way too many

11

investors, from all around the world – each one of them thinking they'll become rich in the cattle business. They can't see the harm they're causing. With too many beeves and overgrazing of the free range, it's going to destroy the market for all of us.'

'You just painted a portrait of Kranston's Continental Beef Consortium,' Reese declared, hooking his thumb towards their newest neighbour. 'By them moving in and laying claim to all of the grazing land west of Lakota creek, it eliminated a lot of extra land we've used in the past to feed our herds. I'm afraid selling off twenty per cent of our cattle won't be enough, not if we have a hard winter.'

Locke ran a hand through his hair. 'Yes, this infernal weather is compounding the problem. It's been the driest year we've had since we started the ranch. Not a single rain shower since early spring.'

'You can add in the wildfires out on the open prairie, too. Most of the range has no grass left at all,' Reese lamented. 'Even the antelope and coyotes have moved off to the mountain ranges.'

'It's the reason for us dumping that last five hundred head of beef on the market. Better to take a loss than watch the animals starve.'

Reese sighed. 'To that end, we're in as good a shape as possible. We've been cutting what grass we could from along the creek and been hauling it over to South Canyon all summer long. I reckon it's our best hope this year. We've kept the cattle out of that basin like always, but it still might not be enough to winter the entire herd.'

'It's a plan that has worked for us in the past, son,' Locke reaffirmed their strategy. 'Never know about Wyoming. We're as prepared as we can be. It's all we can do.'

Reese grunted. 'That idiot Kranston brought in twice as many cattle as the land will support. I'll bet he loses a third of his cattle, even if we have a mild, wet winter.'

'I'm afraid the best years for raising cattle are behind us,' his father said. 'Too many investors and too many beef… the cattle industry is bloated beyond reason. We're all in for a big fall.'

'Thank the Lord for our mining and logging. It might be all that saves us from ruin.'

'How's Lakota creek running?' Locke changed direction.

'Lowest I've ever seen. The cattle have to wade through several feet of mud to reach the trickle of water that's barely running. It's a real concern, with two herds needing it to survive.'

'It's never gone dry before.'

'We can keep our fingers crossed,' Reese said. 'A few well-chosen prayers might also be in order.'

Locke sighed. 'October is almost over and not a drop of moisture. We could sure use a couple good storms to ensure we get some spring grass.'

'Seen several flocks of geese, flying high up, all heading south. Don't recall them leaving so early in the fall. They are usually around until the first good snow.'

'Let's make sure we have enough riders to keep any Kranston cattle from crossing the creek,' Locke spoke with conviction. 'We've been more than fair, allowing them to take control of the fifty square miles of grazing land we used to call our own. We're not giving his company one more inch.'

'Sketcher has been using roving patrols, including Takado and Chayton. They turn back any strays, and the Kranston riders all know better than to push a herd this way.'

13

'That pompous jack picked the worst possible time to settle at Alkali Flats. Even during a good year, it took fifty acres to support each beef out on those plains. He's going to lose his shirt... plus all of the money of his investors.'

Reese sighed. 'I just hope he doesn't drag us down with him.'

CHAPTER TWO

Jared had visited several small towns before he stopped at Deliverance, Colorado. He walked into the sheriff's office and Rod Mason's face lit up in a wide smile.

'Jared!' his bass voice boomed. 'How the heck are you, cousin?'

'I'm surprised to see you sitting behind a desk. Doesn't your wife make you set print for her newspaper these days?'

'Lynette says I'm too clumsy.' He held up his hands. 'Got ten thumbs right here to prove it.' Reaching across the desk the two shook hands. 'It's not a problem' he continued. 'She has a youngster working for her who wants to get into that line of work. It allowed me to concentrate on the chores of a town sheriff.'

'You mean there's enough to keep you busy as a lawman?'

'I'm also Justice of the Peace, and my brother-in-law managed to get me designated as a notary, so I can oversee the exchange of deeds, and rule on contract disputes and little things. Saves us needing a judge most of the time.'

Jared pulled a nearby chair to the desk, sat down, and told Rod all he'd been doing. He finished by admitting he didn't have a single clue as to which town the killer might show up in next.

'Can't stay away from trouble, can you?' Rod remarked, after he had finished. 'I was a little concerned that you nearly got my brother killed a few months back.'

'Cliff never could duck worth a hoot,' Jared joked. 'But he did draw enough fire that I wasn't the only target. If he hadn't been in the fight, I'm pretty sure I wouldn't be standing here now.'

'He writes every few months,' Rod said. 'What about this nanny of his? He mentions her in every letter. Is their relationship serious?'

'The girl is almost eighteen, and the two of them are raising Nessy together. It's pretty much a given that they'll tie the knot after her birthday.'

'He claimed he hasn't chased a girl since he met her. That sure doesn't sound like Cliff!'

'Actually, he's telling it straight. I think he's finally found the girl he's been looking for… and we both know the hound chased everything in a skirt from the time he first discovered girls were different from boys!'

Rod laughed at the accuracy of his remark, then asked: 'Are you going to stay a few days?'

'A couple, at least, so my horse can get some needed rest.'

'Must be tiresome and frustrating, trying to track down a killer with nothing to go on.'

'Yeah, other than taking a hank of hair from his victims, which seems to be his only flaw.'

'I'm thanking you for the warning. I'll keep an eye out for anyone coming through that could be your man.'

'No trouble then? No robberies, murders, mischief of any kind?'

'Not so much.' Rod grew serious. 'And yet…'

Jared was immediately interested. 'I'm listening.'

'There is one chore I don't have time for, a task that requires a superior tracker and expert shot. I know you are the best there is in both departments.'

'Oh-oh,' Jared frowned. 'If you're buttering me up, what kind of spit am I going to be roasting over?'

'It's something you've done before, whereas I haven't got a clue as to how to proceed.'

'If it's milking cows, I am definitely not going to volunteer!'

'No,' Rod assured him. 'It's a cougar, one that's been raising havoc with the little farms and ranches west of town. There's a lot of mountain country that way, and I can't spend several days searching for one particular cat.'

'A mountain lion, huh?'

'It killed a calf, wiped out a coop of chickens, and killed several sheep the other day.' He shook his head. 'This one has developed a taste for killing. It carried off a single lamb for food, yet once it got in among the flock it went on a frenzy that left fifteen woollies dead.'

'Didn't the sheep man have dogs?'

'They were in camp when the cougar hit them. They were on the next hillside.'

'Anyone local who hunts deer or bear with dogs?'

'None that I know of right off, but I haven't had time to do much checking around.'

'OK. Then I'll first try using the sheepdogs. They aren't much good at taking on a cougar, but they might help me find it.'

'I'd sure appreciate it. I'm not as agile since I got shot. Don't know what the bullet hit, but too much exercise causes me some pain in one shoulder and my back.'

Jared laughed a teasing mirth. 'Ole Lightning Rod Mason, tamed by a single bullet and a pretty woman. No one in the family would have believed that before you came to Deliverance.'

Rod showed a good-natured grin. 'Yes, well, you never could best me at any kind of fight. Here's your chance to get one up on me.'

'It's coming on to lunchtime. How about you and Lynette feed me before I make the trip up to where the sheep attack took place?'

'I'll even lend you my horse, seeing as how yours needs a rest.'

'You're too good to me, Rod,' Jared chuckled. 'Cliff would be proud.'

**

Lenard Gauge had four good men and was hard and lean, with a bewhiskered face that appeared to be made of raw-hide. The white in his hair made him look older than his thirty-seven years. Hard living, spending most of his time on the move, he had the flinty eyes of a hawk and a surly yet commanding voice. He paused to survey the saloon, weary of sitting in a corner for over an hour while he and two of his men had slowly nursed a single bottle of whiskey. There were numerous soldiers in the mix of customers, but none of them were spending much money. It was always that way at the end of the month.

'How long until the payroll arrives?' Lazelle wanted to know. 'The boys are getting itchy, and we ain't got enough money to make it more than another two or three weeks.'

Looking at the leader of a second, larger group of men, with whom he had aligned his men for this job, Gauge replied: 'Our sergeant on the inside will let us know when the train is due to arrive. The military often alters transport dates. That way, few people know the exact day when their payroll is arriving.'

'So how much time will we have once the right train pulls into the station?'

Gauge looked at him as if he was stupid. 'A couple hours, like we've been planning, Laz. It's a narrow time frame, but it's what we've been preparing for.'

The somewhat overweight man shook his nearly bald head. 'I don't know,' he complained, his bulldog features wrinkled in a frown. 'It still seems mighty risky, trying to grab an army payroll and rob a bank at the same time.'

'You worry too much, Laz,' Gauge said. 'We've got the men in place – your man, Norris, is working security at the bank, and Hayworth has an inside job at the fort. You and three men take the bank, Branden handles the dynamite, and seven of us steal the payroll. We've got everything planned down to the last detail.'

'I'm worried about the "detail" of the boys in blue who will be hot on our tails,' Elko spoke for the first time in an hour. 'Better pray both jobs go off without a hitch. We're gonna need a good head start.'

'The breed's right,' Lazelle muttered uncertainly. 'One mistake and the air will be filled with lead.'

'Elko used to be a scout. He knows this land better than anyone,' Gauge pointed out to the worrier. 'We make our false trail for the first day or two, then we make a complete turnaround. Once we're headed west, we cut every telegraph line so they can't wire ahead of us. We board the train at Laramie and are off to Utah, Nevada, then all the way to San Francisco. The army won't have a clue as to where to look. We can live the good life and own the town.'

'With winter coming on, the idea of not suffering through snow and cold sounds good,' Lazelle admitted.

'And I hear there are gambling joints and gals aplenty in that waterfront city.'

'You can buy a new gal every night for several months with your share of the money,' Gauge said, showing a wide grin.

'We should be okay,' Elko contributed, striking a positive note. 'So long as we don't get caught in a hard winter storm.'

'Been nary a drop of rain since way last spring,' Lazelle stated. 'Driest fall I ever seen. Not much chance there'll be a lot of snow this year.' He snorted assurance, 'Bet it's the driest winter ever to hit Wyoming.'

***

Darcy Valeron hurried from one place to the next making deliveries from the general store where she worked. Her eagerness was due to it being Saturday, and she always went home after work so as to be with her family on Sunday. It had been a rather large shipment of office supplies and special orders. The last box was special, a baby chair for her cousin Brett's little boy. Rather than go to their house, she took the package to Brett's office. In her haste, she paid no attention to the man who was tying off his mount in front of the jail.

Darcy shifted the bulky package onto her hip and used two fingers to pull the door open a crack. She then inserted her foot so she could flick the door open wide enough to get inside. But taking a step back caused her to bump into the man who had finished securing the reins of his horse. He, also in a rush to get into the sheriff's office, blundered into her, having been unaware of her approach behind him. The collision would not have had any consequence,

20

except that Darcy's foot was still inside the doorway. She was already off balance, and the man – feeling contact – stepped back to avoid her and accidentally trod on the toe of her other foot. She cried out, then made a grab as the heavy package slipped from her grasp. Her flailing arm struck the man in the face! He instinctively jerked away from the blow and his foot missed the edge of the porch. To keep from falling, he automatically latched on to Darcy's arm, with the result that both of them fell over backwards, the man landing on the ground in front of his horse, and Darcy sitting down hard on the walkway. She did manage to avoid landing on the package, but the jolt of landing on her backside caused her to bite her tongue.

She grimaced from the sudden pain and sucked in her breath. While she sat dumbly, with one foot still over the threshold of the sheriff's office, Brett's wife arrived at the entrance to greet her.

'Good gracious! Darcy!' Desiree exclaimed, opening the door wide. 'Whatever are you doing?'

'I'm twying not to cwy,' Darcy lamented, the sting of her injured tongue causing her to use a childish voice.

Desiree bent over to push the package aside, which allowed Darcy to use both hands to straighten her dress and get to her feet.

'I'm right sorry, miss,' the stranger was utterly contrite, having regained his feet. He was covered in trail dust, unshaven, with a haggard look from lack of sleep. 'I didn't see you come up behind me.'

'I about bit off the end of my tongue,' Darcy stammered, still wincing from the pain and blinking back tears. 'Darn, but it hurts.'

'It was totally my fault,' the young man professed. 'I was in a hurry to talk to the sheriff – he's a Valeron, isn't he?'

'I'm Brett Valeron's wife,' Desiree informed the man. 'He should be back in a few minutes.' Then turning back to Darcy. 'Are you sure you are all right, dear?'

She stood there making faces, checking on the condition of her tongue. 'I dan't feel any missing pieces of tongue, so I guess I didn't bite it all the way off.'

'Again, miss,' the gent apologized a second time. 'I'm sure sorry for bumping into you. I had to make a secure knot to hold my mount – she's barely green-broke.'

Darcy frowned and angrily snapped: 'I live on a ranch, buster! I know all too well about being green-broke! I'm also aware that contrary bulls often charge with their eyes shut!'

The man opened his mouth, but Desiree intervened between them, unable to contain her excitement.

'Oh! Is that the new baby's chair? Little Luke is going to love sitting at the table.'

Darcy's defensive posture vanished, smiling at the woman's enthusiasm. 'It's the one you picked out in the catalogue. It just arrived with the afternoon mail.'

'That's wonderful, Darcy. Can you stay and see how it looks after Brett puts it together? He should be back at any time.'

'No, I'm trying to finish early so I can head for home. I'll stop by Monday and see how Luke likes it.' With those words, she lifted the box and handed it to the stranger. 'Here,' she said thickly. 'It's quite heavy, but I know from the experience of our collision that you have the shoulders of an ox.'

The stranger accepted the package and stood obtusely, watching the girl march away. When he tore his eyes off her, he discovered Desiree was studying him.

'Would you be so good as to bring the box inside? My husband can open the package and put the chair together when he returns.'

'Happy to be of service, Mrs Valeron.'

She opened the door wide enough for him to enter. He placed the bundle on the floor next to the sheriff's desk, before releasing a woeful sigh and shaking his head.

'Be-jabbers! I sure didn't mean to run into your attractive friend,' he groaned. 'I was in such a rush… I didn't know she had walked up behind me. And her packing this here box. It must weigh thirty pounds!'

'Why do you want to see my husband?' Desiree remained businesslike. 'Has there been some trouble?'

The man removed his hat, displaying his good manners. 'I was told he was a Valeron. I came here to get directions to the Valeron ranch. I'm on a tight time schedule and it's quite important.'

'Being a Valeron myself, I can help with that.'

The young man's face brightened. 'I'd sure appreciate it, Mrs Valeron, I surely would!'

***

It had been a pleasant Saturday night supper and everyone was finishing the evening by relaxing. Locke Valeron's nephew, Cliff, and his daughter Nessy were with the little girl's nanny, playing a game in the living room. Mrs Valeron was sewing and watching them. As for Darcy, she and her uncle were engaged in a game of chess. On the entire ranch, she was the only one who ever offered Locke a challenge.

'I'm usually gentleman enough not to mention something delicate to a young lady, Darcy,' Locke said, while studying the board. 'But you seem to be moving a bit gingerly this evening.'

She laughed. 'Yes, I sat down rather hard on the walkway in front of Brett's office a few minutes before I left town. Some drifter crashed into me as I was delivering a baby chair to cousin Brett. I was attempting to open the door with my foot, carting the large, heavy package, when he blindsided me. It probably looked comical, because we both ended up sitting on the ground. I about bit off the end of my tongue, so I didn't find it funny at all.'

'Was the fellow daft or completely blind?' Locke inquired. 'A beautiful girl, carrying something bulky... Most men would have hastened to lend you a hand.'

'It was just one of those things. He was clumsy and too focused on where he wanted to go to actually look before whirling about and slamming into me.'

'Could it have been an emergency of some kind?'

Darcy lifted one careless shoulder. 'Dunno. He was looking for Brett. I've never seen the guy before, and he was packing enough dust to fill a grain sack.'

Locke reached out and moved a chess piece. With a grin, 'I've often asked why you hadn't been trying to meet a young man or two. Knocking one of them flat is a technique I hadn't thought of.'

'Very funny, Uncle,' she said, then paused to study the board.

A knock sounded at the front door. Wanetta set aside her sewing and went to see who it was. She returned a few moments later with a man, perhaps in his mid-twenties, with cool, steady hazel eyes and a medium build. He removed his hat to reveal a freshly shorn head of hair, black as coal with a subtle wave at the crown. He wore a gun over a clean suit of clothes, and even his boots had been polished.

Darcy made her chess move before she took notice of the young man. Then her breath caught in her throat.

'You!' she cried. 'What are you doing here?'

'Good day to you a second time, miss,' he replied easily. 'May I say, having your hair down really sets off your features.'

'My features!' Darcy sounded off defensively. 'You mean like a dog having a pointed nose sets off his sharp teeth?'

He displayed a disarming smile. 'I reckon your ready wit can vouch for your sharp teeth, but I was referring to the delicate contours of your face… almost like that of a forest pixie or water sprite.'

She cracked a sly simper. 'Seen of a lot of those have you – pixies and sprites?'

He didn't miss a beat. 'I've seen a couple of nymphs that might qualify.'

'Nymphs?' She raised an eyebrow and frowned at Locke. 'What do you think, Uncle? Is this guy crazy, or has his brain been muddled by peyote or too much hard liquor?'

Rather than retort to Darcy's banter, the fellow took note of the chess game. After studying it for a moment, he smiled and spoke to Locke.

'She thinks she will have you in three moves.'

Darcy gasped at his warning, while her uncle leaned back, a smugness in his expression. 'What else do you see, young man?'

With no lack of confidence, he replied: 'You'll mate her in four.'

'What?!' Darcy cried, rising to her feet and staring at the chess board. 'But…' Then she spotted Locke's strategy. She had set a trap and he had pretended to fall for it, all the while moving in for the kill.

'Of all the lousy, double-crossing…'

'Whoa, Darcy!' Locke exclaimed. 'It's only a game, dear niece.'

'One I'm going to lose!' she fumed. 'I should have seen your plan, you crafty old fox!'

Locke reached out and tipped over his king, then her own. 'Looks like a draw to me.'

'Yeah, right!' she continued to grumble.

Locke turned his attention to the new arrival: 'And now, young man, since you've ruined the game for both of us, what do you want?'

'I've a proposition for you, Mr Valeron. One I hope you'll be interested in.'

'Don't tell me you're a drummer, a salesman of some kind?'

'No, sir.'

'State you name and your business, then. And if you've a few minutes to spare, sit down and show me how good you are at chess.'

'Yes, smart guy,' Darcy growled, before he could reply, taking a step back from the table. 'Put yourself in my chair and let's see you beat Uncle Locke.'

'I couldn't take a seat while you're standing, Miss,' the man said politely.

Sliding over a third nearby chair, the man held it until Darcy had sat down before he took her vacated seat.

'Name's Christopher Roderick,' he introduced himself, 'and I've been helping my father manage our ranch up in Montana. Pa died a short while back, so I have assumed the reins of our enterprise.'

'And for what purpose have you sought me out?' Locke wanted to know.

'I know a little about the Valeron spread, and I have a proposal for you to consider.'

Locke wordlessly placed his chess pieces on the board; Chris began to do the same.

'Suppose we see how good you really are, young man,' Locke said as he made his opening move. 'You win, we'll talk.' He grinned. 'You lose, you walk.'

'Fair enough,' Chris replied. And the game was on.

CHAPTER THREE

Jared had been in the hills for two days, but the sheep-dogs didn't seem to know what they were looking for. He returned them to the herder and began to check the other farms and ranches. His effort was rewarded when a retired army sergeant introduced him to his dog. Lucky was the mutt's name, and he looked to have some bloodhound in him. Rusty coloured, he was bigger than the sheepdogs, with a long nose and floppy ears.

'Lucky is a smart dog,' the sergeant praised. 'I go hunting for rabbits, he finds 'em. If I'm looking for sage hens or pheasants, he'll root 'em out. I took him deer hunting a month or so back, and he sure enough tracked down a six-point buck.'

'This is a cougar,' Jared warned him. 'I don't want him getting too close and maybe get hurt.'

'Lucky has tangled with a bobcat – one got into the shed one night – so he knows big cats have sharp claws.'

'I'd sure like to borrow him long enough to get this rogue mountain lion. He's been doing a lot of damage.'

'Take him to a place where there's been a recent kill,' the sergeant advised. 'He'll pick up the scent and track the animal down.'

Jared heeded his advice, visiting the spot where the numerous sheep had been killed. It had been nearly a week, so he didn't really expect the dog to find anything.

Lucky wandered between the remains of the lion's victims, though most had been pretty much picked over by predatory animals and birds. It took several minutes of him rummaging around before he put his nose to the ground. Then the hound let out an ear-piercing howl and started off in a spirited lope, heading for the nearby mountain range.

Jared kept pace on his borrowed horse, amazed a dog could pick up a scent that was several days old. When they reached the foothills, Lucky changed his pattern, going crisscross along the bottom of a ravine. A quarter-mile up the wash was the rocky face of a sheer cliff, rising a couple of hundred feet into the sky. It was surrounded by a few hardy trees and many slabs of rock and boulders. For a man or dog, much of the landscape was impenetrable, without trails or paths, and there appeared to be a hundred places where a cougar could find himself a den.

Suddenly, Lucky let out another howl, causing Jared's horse to baulk and dance around. The dog had its nose in the breeze and set off at a full run, racing through the underbrush in a mad dash. Jared jerked his horse about and tried to keep pace, but the dog was soon lost in the lower pinon trees and clumps of sage.

Jared pulled his rifle from its scabbard and jacked in a round, but the terrain was too rough for the horse to follow. He stopped and tied off his mount, then took off as fast as his feet could carry him. Unfortunately, his pursuit was hindered by choppy ground, with ridges, obstacles and washes, along with scattered yucca and thick tangles of scrub-brush. He lost sight of Lucky, and was forced to keep track of him by following his excited howls.

The chase wound higher up the coulee, towards the rocky precipice…

Jared caught a glimpse of something, a mere blur going through the brush. He turned that way and charged up the nearest hill, attempting to find a clearing for a shot. He struggled with the footing, but kept going as long as his wind would allow. He began to gasp for air, his lungs were afire, and his heart hammered so hard it shook his entire body. He hoped the lion would go up a tree, as they often did when chased by dogs – such a ploy to escape Lucky would have made him vulnerable for a hunter. Unfortunately this cat chose to head for the safety of its den.

Lucky appeared, hot on the cat's trail, but he was no match for an animal that could take bounds of fifteen to twenty feet at a time. He reached the rocky wall and tried to climb the steep bulwark, struggling for all he was worth. But the ascent was too sheer, nothing but shale rock and stony boulders with no footholds, though Lucky kept trying. Again and again he pulled himself a few feet upwards, but the rock was too steep and his front paws did nothing but scrape and slide, scrape and slide.

Jared finally reached an opening in the cover, but the puma had been too fast and too skilled in its ascent. It was already lost from sight, vanished beyond the lower ledge of the escarpment. Lucky had found the killer lion's den, but he was beyond reach.

***

Gauge met with Lazelle early. There was a cold nip in the air but the sky was clear.

'What's the idea?' Lazelle grumbled. 'Elko 'bout give me apoplexy, waking me up like he done.'

'Does Braden have everything ready?'

'Got it done yesterday, the way we planned.'

'Well, Hayworth sent word. The train is due to arrive tomorrow at noon,' Gauge outlined. 'You need to have your men ready.'

'Right,' Lazelle absorbed the information. 'Two months of preparation are about to be tested. I guess you know, your side of the plan will be the most dangerous.'

'We've got it covered. Once we start our little diversion, the troops will be scrambling like ants after their hill has been stomped by a mule.'

'Still worries me that we didn't get this done last month. Mid-November is not a safe month to travel in Wyoming.'

'Ain't had a single snowflake fall, not even in the mountains. We'll have a clear run.' He shrugged. 'And if we do get a foot or so, a good wind will hide our change of direction. The blue boys will be searching Denver and Kansas City, even the Dakotas. The posse will be chasing their own tail.'

'Still, by starting out the wrong direction, it will take a coupla weeks to reach Laramie, Gauge.'

'We can't take the train until we're sure they've lost our trail. It's why we'll head directly for the Dakotas. If they believe we've doubled back, they'll think we're headed for Denver or Boulder, maybe even Nebraska or Kansas. The last place they'll look is the direction we're going, straight for Laramie.'

'All right. Me and my boys are with you on this. I just hope we've got enough men to pull both jobs at the same time.'

'Braden will join you at the bank as soon as he's done his other chore. He can help with the horses while you get the cash.'

'You've got the bigger job,' Lazelle displayed concern. 'Seven men ain't much of a force against all of the guards and soldiers at the fort.'

'It's all in the plan. With Hayworth being in charge of the armed detail, we won't have any trouble. Soon as we get the strongbox in our care, we make our move and then we're on our way to safety. Once we're clear of the fort, we'll join you and your men. We put the money into pouches and load them on the pack mules. We'll be miles away before anyone can sniff out our trail.'

'Still seems like a lot of things can go wrong, Gauge.'

'It's the way it is,' he shot back. 'The bigger the risk, the bigger the prize.'

Lazelle's frown remained frozen on his face. 'If you're fifteen minutes late, we'll head for safety without you.'

'Agreed,' Gauge gave his okay. 'If something goes wrong and we should get split up, we can meet at Chimney Rock.'

'Fine, but we won't wait more than a day. The same can go for you. We'll each have a pile of loot, so we can take what we have and disappear.'

'That works as an alternative plan. However, unless something goes completely south, we'll meet you at the edge of Cheyenne and make our escape together.'

***

Reese and Sketcher stopped their mounts at the rise overlooking the expansive basin. Below them, several cow hands were driving four hundred head of Hereford cattle to their new home.

'Not much feed down there,' Sketcher observed. 'Most of the grass burned off during the summer. I doubt those cattle can make it more than a week or two on what little is left.'

'Beef of the future – they're supposed to get by on less feed – even sagebrush,' Reese remarked. 'On the plus side, instead of buying more bulls, we have us a fair start on a good-sized herd of Hereford cattle.'

'They better be a tough breed because it's gonna be slim pickings this winter. Their arrival almost offsets the number of cattle on our last drive to market.'

'Kranston should have cut down his herd, too. Most of the cattle watering on his side of the creek are little more than stretched hide over their bones. Snow or not, warm or cold, I'll bet he's gonna lose a hundred head a week from lack of feed.'

'We're in better shape, with the hay stacks over in South Canyon,' Sketcher pointed out. 'But adding another four hundred head?' He heaved a sigh. 'If we get a lot of snow, we'll have to hope we have enough feed to make it through.'

'Silos are pretty full... considering,' Reese contributed. 'The irrigation along the river provided a fair crop of corn. It should help if we get in a bind.' As the comment seemed an end to the food situation, he changed topics. 'You meet any of the riders yet?'

'Only that Roderick fellow. He seems a smart young man.' Sketcher grinned. 'Shane said he actually beat your dad at chess.'

Reese chuckled. 'Earned himself a pat on the back for that feat. I recall the time Brett won a game. My brother bragged about it for a month.'

'Cliff said there were a few sparks between Roderick and Darcy. According to him, the guy held his own when they traded barbs.'

'She's always been headstrong and on the sassy side,' Reese said, describing his cousin. 'I thought taking the job at the general store, she might meet the kind of guy she's looking for.'

Sketcher grunted. 'Sure never gave any of the ranch hands encouragement when it came to courting. I can't recall a single fella she ever took a shine to.'

'What's your thoughts on having a new partner? Pa said that was the arrangement he and Roderick agreed to.'

'Got to be a chore for Martin to figure out,' Sketcher alluded to the accountant/lawyer of the family. 'How's it supposed to work?'

Reese skewed his expression in thought. 'Way I understand it, Roderick will become a ranch foreman, sharing that title with you. I'm to remain the overall ranch manager, so I will coordinate the chores with both of you. As Roderick knows Herefords better than any of us, the hands he brought with him – those who stick after they're paid – will tend to those cattle and also help with anything else we need. Their remuda of horses were in poor shape after the long drive from Montana, so they'll draw from our herd of riding stock.'

'Yeah, but a partner?'

Reese shrugged. 'I've no idea how it's going to work. Everything will be tied to how many cattle we end up with come spring. A hard winter could allow Roderick to own a fair percentage of the herd.'

'I reckon your pa knows what he's doing. He wanted those bulls we bought last year to mix the herd's blood. This will sure enough get that programme running full out.'

'Seems so, Sketch, but keeping most of the bulls for breeding, Roderick won't have hardly any steers going to market. Guess that's why he's a partner instead of Pa trying to buy the herd.'

'Shane was telling me Jared is on a manhunt,' he changed the topic. 'Faro come back from Rimrock without him. The family got a telegraph message from him a couple days ago. He was over at Deliverance. Stopped to visit with

Cliff's brother and Rod hustled him into tracking down a cougar that's been attacking some of the locals' animals.'

'Pa told me a little about that,' Reese stated. 'As for the woman killer he's chasing, the man will have to strike again before Jerry will have a starting point. I recall the newspaper article some time back. It said the perpetrator has killed at least four women, and maybe more.'

'Gonna be a tough chore with cold weather around the corner. Takoda said the signs of a severe winter are everywhere. Hard enough to track a man in good weather. A couple of storms and the trail is lost.'

'Same goes for our ranch. Practically no feed out on the plains, a few feet of heavy snow…' Reese stared down at the herd of red critters. 'Might get a good test of the metal of those beef.'

'And our metal too, Reese, old buddy. I'm crossing my fingers and hoping for a warm, wet winter.'

'Yeah, but I noticed you have a cord of wood stacked up to the roof of your house, along with a full coal bin.'

'Family man has to plan for the worst,' Sketcher said, unable to hide the pride he felt about his wife and four adopted children.

Reese grinned. 'Me and Marie have the shed full of coal too. I don't expect to need another load until the middle of spring.'

'We're lucky men,' Sketcher bragged. 'The Good Lord has blessed our families with this ranch and a good life.'

'Let's pray we don't do anything to lose favour.'

'Amen to that, Reese. Amen to that.'

***

Jared had thanked the sergeant for the use of his dog, but Lucky had scraped a lot of the padding off his front feet, trying to climb solid rock after the cougar. The poor mutt had such tender feet afterwards that Jared had had to carry him home on the back of his horse. It would be a couple weeks before Lucky would be in any shape to hunt the lion again. They had gotten close, but the rocky gorges and steep canyon walls were the cat's sanctuary, and the predatory sheep-killer knew it.

Jared decided a change of plans was his only option. He circulated his idea among the previous victims of the cougar's attacks. He got every person to temporarily move their animals down nearer their house. The sheep were moved to the valley, and even the cattle were driven closer to their respective ranch houses.

Next, he took a fairly young calf and rode up to a place not far from where the mountain lion made its home. He staked the calf in a bit of a vale, low enough that he could keep watch from a rise to either side. After testing the air for direction, Jared chose a position downwind. He left his horse a quarter-mile away and waited until sundown to work his way up to the crest of the hill. He located a sprawling sagebrush to hide his silhouette, one that allowed both cover and view, and laid down a ground blanket. With dusk covering the landscape, he stretched out on the ground and maintained a vigil with his rifle out in front of him.

As predicted, the calf set up a constant holler, mooing for her mother. Jared had something of a reputation as a man with a hair-trigger temper, but not when it came to hunting. He lay there until the moon was full, waiting, watching, rifle cocked, a bullet ready in the chamber.

The calf continued to bawl for several hours, finally lying down to sleep sometime after midnight. When the morning light touched the calf, it was back on its feet, mooing again for its mother and a warm meal.

Jared decided the ploy had been a failure, but it wasn't a waste of time. There was a good chance the cougar had heard the calf, perhaps even came close enough to see it. Instinct probably kept it from making a run at the bait. But maybe after another day of hunger…?

Taking the calf back to its mother, Jared spent most of the day riding back and forth, so as to prevent any deer or antelope from straying into the area. His presence would also discourage the cat from trying to get past him. His eyes burned from lack of sleep, but he only stopped once to eat and grab a couple hours of shut-eye.

That night, he was back to the same place, with a different calf staked out as bait. This time, he felt the puma would be getting good and hungry. It hadn't attacked a domestic animal in several days, so even if it had dragged a partial carcass to its lair, it would be getting anxious for fresh meat.

It was the last night of a full moon. If the cat didn't come this time, Jared would have to use Lucky again. With the sheer rocky mountain at its back door, the chances of getting a good shot at the cougar while it was running from the dog were about the same as getting hit by lightning.

Shortly after midnight the calf suddenly began bawling with a lot more vigour. It began tugging at the rope, dancing about, as if it felt the presence of danger. Jared could feel the breeze in his face, so he knew the prey would not catch his scent. He sighted down the rifle, finger on the trigger. He didn't intend to let the calf be harmed, and that meant taking the shot before…

There! A streaking shadow in the darkness!

Jared judged distance and the animal's speed automatically, squeezing the trigger a moment before the cat could go into its deadly leap!

37

The body of the lion jerked from the bullet's impack and slid across the ground, stopping a few feet away from the terrified calf – which was straining mightily against the rope to get away.

Jared hurried forward, in case the cat was only wounded. To his relief, he discovered the kill shot had been instantaneous, having gone through the cougar's heart. A close inspection of the animal's teeth revealed a tiny fleck of wool. This was the killer puma he had sought. It wouldn't kill any more livestock. Approximately ten feet from nose to tail, and weighing about the same as Jared, this cougar had been one of Nature's most proficient killers.

'Now, Jared,' he said to himself. 'If only you can eliminate the human killer who has been attacking those saloon gals as quickly and easily as this bad boy.'

CHAPTER FOUR

Gauge halted his handful of men, all of them dressed like the regular troopers from the post. He could see the train stopped at the dock and the unloading was under way. His heart was pounding until he wondered if the others could hear it.

'Remember the plan,' he spoke to the others. 'Follow the orders exactly and stay together. If everything goes as planned, we'll be gone without anyone setting off a warning.'

'Sergeant Hayworth better be ready,' Elko warned softly. 'This all comes down to him.'

'It's why he's in for two shares instead of one,' Gauge agreed. 'He's taking the biggest risk. If our plan fails, he will sure enough face a firing squad.'

Elko grunted. 'Once this starts, all of us will be targets.'

At that moment, an explosion sounded that shook the ground. The group of men stood poised until a second blast filled the air. Smoke rose up from a nearby storehouse and splinters of wood showered the surrounding buildings.

'Let's move!' Gauge hollered, leading the way.

Orders were being shouted and troopers were running all directions. The fire crew was hustling about to get the equipment to fight fires, while men were scattered about, many not knowing where to go or what to do.

Hayworth was at the dock, directing his men. The lieutenant overseeing the transfer was baffled and excited, trying to make order out of chaos. Gauge and his men arrived as Hayworth directed the usual payroll guards to help at the closest explosion. That allowed Gauge's detail to move up next to the wagon.

'Move the strongbox to the shed until we get control of the situation!' the lieutenant ordered Haywood, so panicked he paid no attention to the replacement guards. 'Keep it secure until we secure the area!'

Hayworth pointed at Gauge. 'You heard the man! Move this wagon into the Supply Building – on the double!'

Elko jumped up on the wagon seat and headed the team towards the structure. At the same time, Santos and Rogers moved smartly ahead to open the doors. Once inside, the switch was made without delay. Hayworth watched the front of the building, standing guard with Gauge at his side.

A third explosion boomed a short distance away, splintering a vacant warehouse and sending a billowing cloud of smoke into the air. As more men were thrown into confusion, running here or there, Gauge and his men mounted up, ready to ride. Sergeant Haywood commandeered four nearby soldiers and ordered them to accompany the wagon and payroll to headquarters for safety. He took charge of the chore and led the way.

Once the group reached the building, he had the strongbox carted to the empty room used by the paymaster. With the trunk safely in the room, he directed the four men to stand guard until relieved. Telling the men he was reporting to the lieutenant, he left them standing at their posts.

Gauge, dressed as a lieutenant, rode at the head of four troopers and a single pack horse. All were armed, had full saddlebags and rifles at the ready, making their way out of the fort. The guards along the way were more interested in knowing what had happened than where the small detail was headed. Gauge and his party left the fort without having to show the fake orders Hayworth had made for them.

Hayworth, meanwhile, found and informed the lieutenant he had moved the payroll for safe keeping and posted guards. The officer gave him a 'Well done, Sergeant!' and went about trying to restore order. Five minutes later, Sergeant Hayworth was on a horse and headed off from the post to meet up with Gauge.

A few miles away, the Cheyenne bank was being robbed. Norris had got a job working for bank security, and unlocked a back door for Lazelle and the other two men. Braden arrived from setting the explosives to tend the horses, while Lazelle and the others forced the bank manager to open the safe. After emptying it of all the money, gold dust and any valuables, they left the manager tied up alongside a second security guard and were gone.

Lazelle's bank robbers met up with Gauge right on schedule. There was laughter and cheering all around as the bank money was transferred on to the pack mules. Within five minutes, Elko was in the lead, en route to making their false trail. Nothing could go wrong now. They had pulled off the perfect robberies and got away clean. Nothing stood in the way of their escape. Nothing.

Then it began to snow.

***

Jared brushed the snow from his coat and kicked the crusted ice from his boots, before he walked into the

41

Denver police station. A quick look around located the man he wanted. Sergeant Fielding was pouring himself a cup of coffee at the stove. The man glanced over his shoulder, saw him, and uttered an exaggerated groan.

'I thought the clouds were darker than usual this morning. I should have known trouble was at my door.'

Jared laughed at the comment. 'I'm not here to arrest or kill anyone, Sergeant. I'm in need of some help, and it's in your best interest.'

'Every time you show up for my help, I risk losing my job… or my life.'

'This time it's information only.'

He paused. 'You want a cup of sludge? This stuff will put some hair on your chest.'

'I had breakfast before I stopped by. I'll pass.'

Fielding made his way over to his desk and nodded to a vacant chair nearby. Jared pulled the chair over and sat down across from him.

'Give me the bad news, Valeron. Who we looking for this time?'

Jared removed the local paper's account of the murder from several weeks back. He laid it out so the article was facing up, and asked: 'Any clues about this gal's murder yet?'

'We have nothing,' Fielding grumbled the answer. 'No one saw anything, heard anything, or knows anything. We talked to every person working at the saloon, but no one remembered seeing anyone leave with the gal. She was there one minute and gone the next. Bartender's helper found her when he was cleaning up the trash in the back alley. They haul the garbage off once a week to a dump site out of town.'

'I've been to Junction City and Leadville following the killer's trail. They told the same story at both places. I've checked hotels and rooming houses for matching names, talked to the liveries and stables… it's gotten me nothing but saddle sores and a headache that won't quit.'

'Part of being a lawman,' Fielding said flatly. 'What can I do to help?'

'How about a list of names from the hotels at the time of the murder? Have you also talked to the livery, the general store owners, and everyone else about any travellers coming through?'

'We interviewed every man, woman and child we could think of, from church leaders to the ladies on the Civic Improvement committee. The killer didn't get noticed by anyone. He somehow managed to get Trixie alone, then strangled her and stashed her body among the rubbish.'

Jared heaved an abject sigh. 'Without a trail to follow, I'm about as much good as a one-legged jack rabbit at a jumping contest.'

'I'm sorry I have nothing to help,' Fielding said. 'We turned over every rock and tin can in the entire city – from here to Golden – and found absolutely nothing.'

'Have to wonder where the killer will hold up, what with these continuous storms.'

'Snowing every day like it is, they are talking the possibility that even the trains might stop running. Guess the drifts are piling up pretty deep in the canyons or ravines. The way it snows a foot, melts an inch and re-freezes, it's making it hard to keep anything moving.'

'I spoke to the guy at the express office. They have dozens of orders backed up for shipping, but the stage and freight outfits can't move, either.'

'Did you look at some of them as suspects?' Fielding asked. 'Maybe a stage guard or driver has been involved in these killings.'

'The distance between attacks is too far for an ordinary stage hand. The killer might be using the stage and railroad both; he might be travelling alone – it's impossible to know. I hate the fact of the matter, but our single option is to wait until he strikes again and hope he leaves a trail to follow.'

'What are you going to do next, Valeron? You going to take up residence here and wait?'

'There's other things I can do. When I checked at home, Dad wired back that brother Nash is running low on provisions. In fact, with the stage and freight companies sitting idle, everyone living in Castle Point is short of supplies. I thought I might pick up a couple of mules and haul what I can.'

'Sure don't seem to be letting up,' the sergeant observed. 'Every time I look out the window, it's nothing but snow and more snow. Check the walkways – there's six feet of snow stacked along it, and mountains of it piled high in every alleyway.'

'While I wait for the weather to break or not from the storms, I'll get a room and rest my horse for a day or two. After that, I'll check with Nash and see what the town and him need the most.'

'I'll spread the word around,' Fielding offered. 'If you decide to try and haul some supplies up to your brother, there might be a teamster or cowpoke in town who is broke enough to make the trip with you.'

'Thanks, Sarge. Two or three of us could haul a lot more freight than me alone.'

***

Shane Valeron rode up to the Indians, his horse moving slowly as it was having to traverse three feet of snow on the ground. The pair of Lakota ex-army scouts were bundled up against the cold, with ponchos to keep off the endless deluge of snowflakes.

'Twenty-six days in a row, we've gotten snow,' Shane opened the conversation. 'I've never seen it come down like this before. Latest news said there were snow storms throughout North Texas and even a few inches fell in San Francisco.'

Takoda tipped his head in an affirmative gesture. 'It's the same for us. When we were chasing some Cheyenne up north with the soldiers, we got snowed in for a week. But then the storm quit for several days and we made it back to the fort. Never seen it come down like this for so many days at a time.'

'And cold as lake bottom,' Chayton tossed in one of his rare comments.

'The cattle are floundering like landlocked fish in a drying-up pond,' Shane observed. 'If we don't get a break soon, they are going to start dropping from lack of food.'

'No trees for bark, and very hard to eat sagebrush,' Takoda replied. 'We never used our winter hay before in the month of December, but this time…'

He didn't have to continue, so Shane speculated: 'I'll bet Kranston is pacing the floor day and night. Bringing in ten thousand head of cattle, trying to feed them on half the amount of prairie that many head requires – the guy is going to lose his entire herd if the weather doesn't let up.'

'Sad for cattle, not for Kranston,' Chayton made the statement.

'We stopped some of his riders from pushing a herd towards our western flatland two days ago,' Takoda informed Shane. 'Told them it was a waste of time. We had already moved our cattle from that area because there wasn't a blade of grass left to be found.'

45

'Well, the only good thing about this snow is that we don't have to keep men posted to guard South Canyon or our stacks of hay. Can't move a wagon with this much snow, and the Kranston herd would never survive a drive that far.'

Another rider appeared, and seeing them perched on the rise, rode in their direction. As he came closer, Shane recognized Christopher Roderick, the recently added junior partner to the Valeron ranch. He pulled up as he reached the trio and tipped his hat to remove an inch of accumulated snow.

'I thought I was moving my herd to warmer territory,' he said, flashing a roguish simper. 'This beats the most snow we usually get in Montana in an entire winter.'

Shane gave a negative bob of his head. 'Reports say that part of the country is buried under even more snow than us.'

'Gonna be a big loss of cattle if we don't get some relief, and soon.'

'Speaking of the weather, how are those odd-looking critters you brought here holding up?' Shane queried.

'Hereford beef have wintered in parts of the world where no other cattle can survive. They seem to thrive where ordinary cattle starve or freeze.'

'I did notice they are not as prone to clustering in bunches for warmth,' Shane acknowledged. 'A good many cattle suffocate from crowding together when it gets stormy or cold.'

'Yeah,' Chris agreed. 'Best of all, Herefords can live on sagebrush, scrub oak or tree bark. Nothing fussy about their diets.'

'More like a herd of goats than cattle,' Takoda chipped in.

Shane pulled out his timepiece and looked at it. 'I guess I know where you're headed.' He chortled in a teasing fashion. 'Darcy comes home on weekends, and this is Saturday.'

Chris displayed a sheepish grin. 'Temple worries about her with the trails being completely covered.'

'What a thoughtful guy you are, to volunteer to ride all the way to Valeron and see she gets home safely!'

'That's me – Mr Thoughtful.'

'Me think him want Miss Darcy for his woman,' Chayton spoke up. 'He maybe not know her much.'

Takoda and Shane laughed at the usual taciturn Indian's statement. Chris also bobbed his head in agreement but retorted: 'I always enjoy a challenge, Chayton.'

'Want challenge – wave stick to turn stampede… better chance you live.'

Takoda looked at Shane. 'What do you think? Chayton is beginning to sound like an ordinary ranch hand.'

Shane shook his head in amazement. 'I've known you boys since I was a kid. Today is possibly the most I ever heard Chayton speak in one sitting.'

Chris straightened in the saddle and glanced skywards. 'Still coming down,' he said, referring to the falling snow. 'Guess I'd better get a move on. Darcy doesn't refuse my company, but then, I've never been late arriving either. I can't be sure she'll wait.'

'Plan your strategy like you were playing Uncle Locke at chess,' Shane advised. 'Because one wrong move…' He drew a line across his throat.

Chris laughed, lifted a hand in farewell, and started his horse moving towards the main trail leading to town. At least, he headed for where the buried trail used to be. Covered in several feet of snow, the landscape was more an

47

ocean of white, with undulating waves where the wind had blown drifts. Fortunately, on this particular day, the wind was not gusting, maintaining a steady breeze of only a few miles per hour. It was difficult and cold, but not anything like actual blizzard conditions.

'Has your sister said anything to you about the new man chasing her skirt?' Takoda asked Shane, as the three of them watched Christopher ride away at a steady walk.

'She doesn't confide in me about such things,' Shane answered. 'In the man's defence, she hasn't tried to contact Jared to complain about unwanted attention.'

'Not yet!' Takoda grunted. 'But the new foreman better not make a mistake… not even one.'

***

Lazelle left the table where he and Norris had been playing chequers. He strode over to the bar-room table where Gauge, Elko and Hayworth were sitting. They'd been playing cards, but had become sullen and silent, each of them sick of being idle and worried about their future.

'Another six inches last night and still snowing,' he grumbled, pulling out a chair. He paused to pour himself a drink from the half-empty bottle, threw his head back and gulped the liquid in one swallow.

'I think this came from a sick horse,' he muttered, pulling a face as he sat down.

'Being snowed in the way we are, it might have come from a stray dog,' Hayworth quipped. 'Tasted better stuff when one of the guys in the barracks made booze from potatoes. Let me tell you, that curled the hair in your ears.'

'Got another complaint from the town fathers,' Lazelle said, keeping his voice down. 'This tiny burg ain't set up to support a dozen extra men all winter long. Even the stage didn't make it through this past week.'

'If the snow would just let up, we'd pull out,' Gauge complained. 'Damn it all! We can't head across country during a snowstorm that might stack up five- or six-foot drifts and no way to see the trails.'

'With the world buried in white up to our necks, many of the landmarks aren't visible,' Elko pitched in.

'We could head towards the railroad tracks and follow the rails,' Hayworth flipped out the idea. Gauge nixed the notion: 'Gets much worse and the trains won't be able to keep running.'

Lazelle hit the tabletop with his fist. 'Well, we've got to do something! These people are running out of supplies, and paying our way is using up a lot of our cash. It's not what we planned.'

'It wouldn't do us no good to take over this dirt-water town, Laz. Even if we did, there isn't enough food to get us through another month.'

'Your plan to pussy-foot around with the soldiers has cost us the best travel time during the whole damn month!'

'Can I help it if the worst snowstorm anyone can remember happened to hit the day we left Fort Russell?'

'What I'm saying, Gauge, is that we're further away from San Francisco than when we started. Everything we do costs us time and money!'

The overall leader of the gang furrowed his brow in thought. 'We only have to make it as far as Laramie. From there, we take the first train headed west and never look back.'

Lazelle snorted his disdain. 'With all this snow, you're talking a two-week ride. Mostly because we wasted several days making our fake trail going the wrong way.'

'What if we make for Boulder or another town along the railroad line?' Hayworth suggested. 'We could split up, a couple men here, another three or four there. You know, make it look like there ain't a dozen of us arriving in town at one time.'

Lazelle turned down that idea. 'There'll be wanted posters for us everywhere by now, and Boulder has a police force. For all we know, there might be lawmen or troopers sitting and waiting for us at every train station for a hundred miles.'

Gauge waved a dismissive hand. 'We can cut the telegraph wires before we get to Laramie. After this much time, no one will be looking for a few cowboys who are out of work. I mean, there'll be dozens of them on the move when the cattle start dying from this endless snow.'

'Or those punchers who are fed up freezing their cans trying to save a few critters,' Hayworth tossed in his thoughts.

Gauge mused: 'So, what we need is a place that doesn't have any law, and can be cut off from the world by cutting a couple of their telegraph wires. Then we can wait out the storm without worry about the army or a posse.'

'No posse is going to be after us still, not with a full month of snowfall!' Elko declared. 'They've no trail to follow.'

'We don't want to reach Laramie and have to sit around if the trains stop running,' Lazelle said. 'Too risky to spend any more time in that place than we have to.'

'They are toughing it through, so far,' Gauge said. 'And we can board in small groups, like Hayworth suggested. There might be a few soldiers billeted there, but we can make sure they don't take notice of us.'

'What lies between us and Laramie?' Lazelle asked Elko.

The ex-scout thought for a bit. 'The old Mormon Trail, the railroad line, even the pony express route come together up that way. I recollect there's a little burg between Laramie and Cheyenne. It serves the pilgrims and travellers, along with a few small ranches or farms.'

Gauge was interested. 'Is it big enough to put up the dozen of us for a week or two?'

'Let me think…' Elko searched his memory. 'Yeah!' His eyes lit up. 'The town is called Castle Point. Been some time since I went that way, but it didn't have a lawman or jail. It's mostly a few stores and a saloon that serve the pilgrims and drovers. There are a couple small ranches thereabouts, too.'

'I know the place!' Hayworth exclaimed. 'I rode with a patrol through there a year or so back. There was no bank, and it didn't look very prosperous. We didn't stop except to water the horses.'

'How far do you figure it is from here?' Gauge asked the two men.

'No more than forty miles,' Hayworth answered. 'There's a stage out of Cheyenne that goes through, but they won't be moving until this storm lets up. Travelling in snow this deep, a team would be spent in five miles. No way would they make their usual station.'

'If *they* aren't moving, how are *we* supposed to manage a trip that far?' Lazelle growled.

'We rotate lead riders,' the ex-scout replied. 'Two or three horses would break trail for those behind for a mile or two, then the ones from the rear would take their place. By constantly switching them over, we should make fifteen to twenty miles a day.'

'And at nights?' Lazelle continued to grill his idea. 'How do we keep us and the horses from freezing?'

Elko said: 'There's a way station for the stage lines, but it's run by a couple'a families and they might be on the lookout for us.'

'A better overnight stop would be the trading post over the way,' Hayworth suggested. 'We can stop early or ride late to reach that place for shelter. It isn't much, but it would do for a single night.'

'Anything is better than here,' Lazelle snorted. 'When do we move?'

'The first clear day we get,' Elko volunteered. 'With any luck, we can make it to Castle Point before any new storms hit. The people here don't want us, but they know we can't leave until the snow stops falling.'

Gauge gave a nod of approval. 'Pass the word – we leave the first clear morning we get.' Then focusing his gaze on Elko: 'You and the sarge pick up a couple of extra mounts and whatever else we're going to need. Soon as we reach Castle Point, we'll rest the animals for a few days and hope the trains are still running by the time we get to Laramie.'

'Let's do it,' Lazelle said. 'I'm sick to death of this part of the country!'

CHAPTER FIVE

Jared sent a wire to Nash asking how their little town was faring. The reply said the general store was desperate for supplies as both the stage and freight companies were unable to buck the snow to get there. He then checked at the depot and express company to see how much stuff was ready to be shipped to Castle Point. Both places had freight scheduled for the town via Cheyenne. However, Cheyenne's express companies were faced with the same problem – cargo was piling up and they didn't want any extra until it could be shipped.

Jared went by the police station, but Fielding told him no one had stopped by to volunteer for the arduous journey he planned. Rather than delay any longer, he decided he would pack as much as he could and hope it was enough to get the little burg through. It might be weeks before there was enough of a thaw to allow the freight wagons to start moving again.

It didn't take long to surmise this would be a big undertaking. There was sufficient product to fill a box car or three or four freight wagons. Even setting aside nonessentials and items that would freeze and be useless, he had a major chore on his hands.

As he was making a list and stacking the most necessary items on one side of the freight warehouse, a grizzled
brute of a man approached him. About half again the size
of Jared, he had an unkempt beard that reached his collar-
bone and made him look older than his years. He wore the
heavy clothes of a stage or freight driver, and atop his head
was a fur cap with ear-flaps tied at the top.

'Mr Valeron,' he greeted, his eyes bright and steady. 'I
was told that some crazy son is planning a mule train type
operation all by his own self. I wanted to have me a look at
the yahoo who would try something so insane.'

'I'm the yahoo,' Jared replied. 'And I reckon them that
know me best have always doubted my sanity.'

'So, it ain't enough that you're gonna commit suicide
yourself – you've been asking about to hire someone dumb
enough to buck six-feet snow drifts and die with you?'

Jared grinned. 'I don't suppose you know anyone that
short of smarts, do you, friend?'

The fellow laughed, in rather infectious mirth, as if he
readily enjoyed a good guffaw. 'Truth is, I had me a heart-
to-heart with Sergeant Fielding. He claims this is a mission
of mercy. People might starve or need medicine and such.
I figure he was playing on my compassion for others.'

'And do you have a compassion for others?'

Another laugh. 'Not me, Valeron. What the lawman
offered was a deal in exchange for a ten-day jail sentence.
One of my sins is a weakness for liquor. I kind of drank up
the last of my money, then asked politely for credit.'

'And when the bouncer threw you out?' Jared inquired.

'I give him a right pretty black eye.' He shrugged. 'Next
thing, I'm cold sober and sitting in a cell, being told I'll
be on the working end of a shovel clearing snow from
walkways for the next ten days.'

'That would be a whole lot safer than the journey I'm about to undertake.'

'I can maybe help with that,' the man said. 'I'm an independent freighter, see? But these endless snowstorms have shut down me and my wagon. That said, my draught horses are sturdy and well fed. I figure I can ride one and lead the other three, lessen' you want to rent me a horse. That would give us four sturdy pack horses, and they've done a share of hauling that way. I often deliver back to places where a wagon can't go.'

'It's going to be a tough haul, but I need to get started. The train will get us as far as Cheyenne, so we only have to travel another two days to reach Castle Point.'

'I don't want to sound unsympathetic or like I'm taking advantage of a bad situation, but I've been stuck here so long that I'm flat broke.' He hurried to add: 'I mean, the ten days in jail was going to be free room and board, but I can't afford to work for nothing. I need to earn enough to get by until I can move some freight.'

'I'm doing this for free, because my brother is the town doctor and needs some medical stuff. You can count on earning the entire payment for the freight we haul to the other stores. I'll toss in the rent for a good horse. That way, with your team and the two pack mules I rented, we ought to be able to haul the equivalent of a full wagon.'

'How long do you figure?'

'I'd like to be there by Christmas.'

'Should make that easy enough,' the gent figured in his head. 'When we leaving?'

'Another day or two to line up a boxcar for the animals and supplies,' Jared outlined. 'Take the train to Cheyenne and it's should only take two to reach Castle Point.' With a grin, 'Ought to be a piece of pie.'

'Frozen pie,' the fellow joked. 'My name's Payne' – and he spelled it, flashing a crooked grin. 'My ma used to call me the biggest *pain* in her life… kind of a play on words.'

'My folks have called me the same on numerous occasions… and it's spelled exactly like the usual word.'

'What do you need from me?' Payne asked.

'I've ordered the liveryman to make some protective cow-hide wraps for the horses. We'll strap them tight from fetlock to knee. There's so much ice buried under the snow, wading through it would take the hide right off their legs.'

'Well, I've got some of them for my horses already. I've been caught in a few storms before. When the snow turns to ice, got to protect your animals' legs. My leggings are treated buffalo hide, and they work just fine.'

'In that case we'll finish organizing this stuff and take a look over at the dock warehouse. I've been stacking everything that needs to go next to the door. Since you're more familiar with hauling freight, it'll be your job to figure how much each animal can carry. We'll sort out as much as we can take at the dock warehouse, and add it to this stuff. When we have it all lined out, I'll rent us room in a boxcar, both for the freight and the animals.'

'Whatever you say, Valeron. From now on you're the boss!'

***

Chris helped with the loads of hay and grain. Unable to use wagons, several men pulled makeshift sleds or travois behind their horses. The cattle were in pockets, floundering in snow that was belly deep and trapped by drifts six to eight feet high. It made getting to them a monumental chore. However, once they became aware of the feed being provided, they used every bit of their strength to get to it.

Other cowhands used picks and shovels to bust through the ice so the cattle had water. Trails were made through the icy crusts so the trapped animals could reach both feed and water. When finished each day, men and horses would retire to beds and the barn, regaining strength for daylight and another day of battling Nature's fury.

Shane and Chris ended up in the canyon together, distributing sleds of grain for the Hereford cattle. The two of them paused after emptying their sleds, watching the animals clean up the last specks of grain.

'Got to admit, Roderick,' Shane observed. 'Your beef are in far better shape than the rest of the herd. And that's saying something, considering you drove them all the way from Montana several weeks back.'

'They are the beef of the future,' Chris declared. 'Your uncle Locke foresaw this day when he started buying Hereford bulls.'

'Might be the only cattle that survive, if we run out of feed.'

'Takoda mentioned you had a couple silos of corn, if needed. If we can get through the next two months, March should bring a good crop of spring grass. All this snow is bound to help turn the drought around.'

'Yeah, but only if we have cattle left to enjoy the rewards.'

Chris removed his glove and pulled out his pocket watch. 'What the…?' Then he shook the timepiece and popped it against his gloved hand. 'My watch has stopped. I didn't realize it when I checked it a while ago. What is the actual time?'

Shane looked skyward at the clouds. 'Can't see the sun. Must be getting on to late afternoon. Let me get my watch.' He removed a glove and did some digging inside his coat, until he could finally get the ticker out and look at it.

'Uh-oh, you're running late, son. Being Saturday, Darcy is gonna be leaving in about an hour. With all this snow, it'll take you twice that to make it to town from here.'

Chris unhooked the towing rope for the sled and tossed it to Shane. 'Hope the snow holds off until I catch up with her.'

'Good luck!' Shane hollered, as Chris started his horse out of the canyon.

Looking skyward, the day had been fairly quiet, little wind and an occasional flurry, but there was an ominous bank of clouds settling over the valley. If it started to storm….

***

Darcy had finished for the day. She groaned as fresh snow began to fall. Would these despicable storms never quit? The gusting winds had blown enough snow to completely fill in the coulees and ravines. There was news of a thick white blanket of snow and ice covering the entire country, from Texas to the Dakotas and throughout the mid-west. Freight wagons, stage coaches and even some of the trains were unable to cope with the mountains of snow. It seemed there was no end in sight.

Bundling up, Darcy made her way to the livery. The pathways had snow piled high to either side, and still she had to wade through several inches. A cold wind chose that moment to hit her with a spray of ice crystals from out of the north. She didn't doubt the land would get another few inches of snow before morning… again.

'You're horse is saddled, Darcy,' the liveryman said. 'Are you sure you want to ride out with this icy blow comin' in? From the looks of the clouds, it could be fixing to really cut loose.'

Darcy thanked Stubby, then put up a hand to shield her eyes from the irksome snow. 'Isn't Christopher... uh, Mr Roderick,' she corrected. 'Hasn't he arrived in town yet?'

'Been keepin' watch, but he ain't showed.' With a concern etched into his face, 'Mayhaps you should wait a bit.'

'He knows what time I get off work,' she countered curtly. 'I'll probably meet him on the trail before I've gone a mile.'

'I'd feel a mite better if he were here,' Stubby voiced his worry. 'With the wind picking up and new snow coming down, you ain't going to be able to see three feet in front of you.'

'I know the trail well,' Darcy dismissed his warning. 'I'll be fine.'

Stubby held the bridle to her mount until she was aboard. Then he handed her the reins, waved, and returned to the protection of the barn.

Darcy turned her horse into the storm and started moving. She wasn't afraid of getting lost. She made the trip every week. As for the mare she was riding, she had been born at the ranch; she ought to know the way home.

***

'There she is...' Hayworth announced. 'I told you there was a trading post near the river. Been here for years.'

'No telegraph wires,' Lazelle took note. 'That's good.'

'The pair of old coots running it used to be trappers. They don't keep a lot of goods on hand, but we can spend the night. Sleeping on the floor beats bedding down in a snowbank.'

'Between you and Elko, we've got the best guides a man could hope for,' Gauge praised the two men. 'I never doubted either of you for a minute.'

'Let's not pat each other on the back too hard,' Lazelle grumbled. 'My hands and feet are blocks of ice. If them two old warts decide they won't give us shelter from this storm, I couldn't even draw my gun.'

'Money talks their language,' Gauge assured him. 'I'll show them twenty bucks and they'll turn the place over to us.'

'Our loot ain't going to last if we keep spending it like water in every burg or lodge we come across.'

'It's the only leverage we have, Laz. Killing people draws a lot of attention.'

'So does a dozen riders with spending money,' he shot back. 'The cowhands that are being put out of work because of this endless snow will be lucky to have a dime to spend. Ranchers watching their herd of cattle dying aren't gonna pony-up much money for the men they've had to let go.'

'Let's see how helpful these two are going to be,' Gauge offered.

Laz growled, 'If they give us any guff we'll toss them in a snowbank and let the cold and ice take care of them.'

Elko grunted. 'Can't imagine why I never wanted a trading post of my own. I'd likely have ended up in the same fix as the two gents we are about to visit.'

'If the snow doesn't get any worse, we'll set out first thing in the morning,' Gauge said. 'No need to do any harm if this goes smoothly.'

'They can contact the army quick enough,' Lazelle warned.

'There's no telegraph for miles around,' Elko said. 'If we don't give them a reason to turn rat on us, they won't be in any hurry to talk to anyone about us.'

Lazelle shook his head. 'Damned if you ain't getting soft, breed.'

60

'Clever is the word,' Gauge argued. 'Leave them with a little money and in a few days it won't matter what they tell anybody. We'll be out of this part of the country.'

'We'll see how it goes,' said Lazelle, making no promises.

***

A gust of swirling ice crystals blinded both horse and rider. With the heavy cloud cover hugging the earth it was nearly dark. Chilled to the bone and unable to get a fix on her direction, Darcy was beginning to regret her dogged determination to make the ride home on her own. Stopping the horse, she reached down and brushed away the crusted ice that clung to the hair around the animal's eyes.

'What do you think, Cinnamon?' she asked the game little mare. 'Should we turn back?'

However, the way behind her was as black a void as it was in front. Darcy had no idea if she was closer to the town than she was to the ranch. When Christopher had been riding with her, it had taken no more than two hours to make the ride. She had been battling the trail for at least that long already, and had no idea how much further she had to go.

In a moment of grim uncertainty she removed the glove on her right hand and dug out the small .32 calibre pistol from her handbag. She warned Cinnamon to be 'steady' and fired the gun into the air.

The mare jumped at the sudden noise, but the wind and snow stifled the blast, as if the gun's muzzle had been covered with a pillow. Darcy doubted the sound travelled more than a few hundred feet. Even so, she stuck the gun into her coat pocket. She would shoot off another round every fifteen minutes, just in case Christopher was close enough to hear. She knew he would be looking for her, and was growing more and more concerned that they hadn't met on the trail. If he had been running late, wouldn't he have used the normal route?

'Yes,' she muttered, 'if I'm anywhere near the main trail!' Everything looked the same – no hills or mountains, everything mingled together in an endless, tempestuous ivory sea. With darkness covering the land, the temperature was falling. Only a few degrees below freezing at the moment, it would soon dip to zero or below. If she didn't get home in the next hour or two…

Darcy swallowed her regret. She couldn't allow thoughts like that to enter her head. If she panicked, she could die.

***

It had been snowing hard by the time Chris reached town. Taking the shortest route had saved a mile or more, but he quickly regretted his choice. Stubby informed him that Darcy had left thirty minutes earlier. Silently cursing his lateness and her stubborn independence, he started after her, barely able to pick out the indentations of her trail. Regrettably, the wind whipped the heavy snow about so quickly it soon covered any trace of her horse's tracks.

Between the impending dusk, the thick, low-hanging clouds and the ever blasting winds, Chris could only guess the location of the trail. One thing in his favour, he had been born with a dead reckoning that surpassed most others he had ever met. It was a blessing he had taken for granted, always knowing which way to go, with or without landmarks. Even with the trail covered and the world around him buried in a three-foot blanket of freezing snow, he could have made it back to the ranch without too much trouble.

Unfortunately, he didn't know if Darcy had remained on the trail or if she was now lost. He pressed on, one hour… then two. The world was completely encompassed by swirling beads of ice and a brutal thirty-to-forty mile-per-hour wind. Total darkness had come early, and it was growing colder by the minute. If he didn't find her soon….

He suddenly pulled his horse to a stop and listened. Had that been a muted pop? Perhaps from a small calibre gun?

He strained his ears but could hear only the howling of the wind. Rather than sit there blindly searching the blackness, he pulled his own gun. Patting his horse on the neck to calm him, he fired off a round and then remaining completely still, waiting, using his keen sense of hearing.

Faintly, another pop went off. He felt certain it was to his right and urged his horse in that direction. To prevent losing contact by going the wrong way, he lifted his weapon and squeezed off another round.

A few seconds later, the answering gunshot sounded – it was closer! He tried to coax more speed from his horse, but it had little more to give. It had been toughing it out against drifts and deep snow since early morning and was nearly spent.

Through the gloom, Chris spotted the blurred figure of a horse and rider. He held his breath, fearful it would be a lost traveller or cowhand. Drawing close enough to make out the rider, he experienced a great wave of relief.

'Miss Valeron!' he shouted. 'Over here!'

She didn't call back, remaining steadfast, wrapped up in a blanket that was caked with snow and ice. As he pulled up within reach, he could almost see the fire in her eyes.

'Mr Roderick! Where the devil have you been?' she demanded to know. 'I've shot up all of my ammunition… down to my last two bullets!'

'I'm sorry, but…'

'I can't feel my feet – I think they're frozen,' she continued to rant. 'Even my eyelashes have ice in them. I've never been so cold and miserable in my entire life!'

'Miss Valeron, I…'

'What took you so long to find me? Have you been lost all this time?'

'You're off the trail by a half-mile,' Chris finally rebuked her ire. 'Why didn't you wait for me?'

'You weren't there! You were late!'

'My watch stopped. I didn't realize how late it was. Shane and I were…'

'Mr Roderick,' her voice held a dire warning. 'I don't want to hear anything about your day. Just tell me you know where we are and that you can get us home.'

'I'd guess we're no more than a mile from the ranch,' he replied. 'If the horses don't give out, we should be there in about thirty minutes.'

'T-then s-s-stop talking,' she accented the fact she was shivering. 'Take me home!'

'My horse is almost played out. You'll have to break trail for us or he won't make it.'

'Just point me in the right direction,' Darcy said. 'Cinnamon wants to go home, too.'

A little over thirty minutes later, they arrived at the ranch.

Temple and Gwen were both at the door when Darcy stopped her horse at the front of her house. Temple hurried out to his daughter and physically pulled her out of the saddle. He took her in his arms like a small child.

'Dear girl!' Gwen cried, placing a hand on Darcy's arm. 'We've been worried sick about you.'

'Blame it on my escort,' she muttered. 'But get me to the fireplace.'

As Temple carried her into the house, Gwen remained for a moment, her arms wrapped about her chest to fight the chill. 'Christopher?'

'Your daughter can fill you in. I've got to get these two animals to the barn. They're both going to need a dose of whiskey and a full helping of oats. Then I'll have to rub them down and toss a blanket over them. Otherwise we might lose them both.'

'What about you?' she asked. 'You must be about frozen, too.'

'I hail from Montana, Mrs Valeron. This is pretty much a normal winter for me.'

'Well, thank you for seeing our daughter home… and good night,' she ended their meeting.

As she fled back to the warmth of their house, Chris took a moment to glance skyward. Squinting against the constant peppering of hard snow pellets, he whispered: 'Thank You, Lord,' his voice full of sincere reverence. 'I couldn't have found her without You pointing me in the right direction. I'm beholden to You for her safety, and hope she bounces back with no permanent ailments. Amen.'

CHAPTER SIX

The lieutenant watched as Jared and Payne loaded their pack animals. He and two other troopers had met the train and talked to each and every passenger, interrogating them with questions about any suspicious units or gangs of men.

'So these fellas robbed the Cheyenne bank and stole your monthly payroll at the same time?' Jared summed up what he'd been told. 'That speaks of brass and brains.'

'We figure there were no fewer than ten men... maybe a dozen.' He made a helpless gesture. 'I was double-crossed by one of my own sergeants. He slipped in several phony soldiers during the disarray caused by three explosions. We didn't know the money box had been replaced with a fake one until the paymaster opened it the next day. It held a handful of newspapers, and Sergeant Hayworth was missing as well.'

'Sounds like quite a haul for the bandits.'

'It's why we've been asking everyone we run across if they've seen a group of men with a lot of money to spend in the past couple of weeks.'

'Money's tight, so they'd stand out from most,' Jared observed. 'But I don't gamble all that often, so I wouldn't have seen them. Plus, I've been trying to get a lead on a perverted swine who has strangled several dance-hall gals around the country. I didn't give any special notice to groups of men, as I've been looking for a lone killer.'

'Men with that much money would sure enough head out of the country,' Payne chipped in his opinion on the subject. 'Shucks! Look at the job I've hired on for… just to keep from starving.'

The lieutenant chuckled. 'If you get hit with a major blizzard, no one is going to find your frozen bodies until the spring thaw.'

'You give a man a real boost with that kind of talk,' Payne jawed back. 'No wonder your sergeant up and doublecrossed you.'

Jared paused to catch his breath from securing another box. 'You've no idea where those varmints got off to?'

'We were only able to follow their trail a few miles. They were headed for the Dakotas, but we lost the trail after the third day of heavy snow. Being hit with endless storms day after day, we had to turn back.' He shrugged. 'Can't follow a trail that's been covered with two or three feet of blowing snow.'

'Tell you one thing, Lieutenant,' Jared made the observation, 'if I was flush with cash, the last place I would go is the Dakotas. I'd wager they were making a fake trail to hide the true direction they intended. They likely turned south once they figured they'd lost you.'

'I'd be thinkin' that way too,' Payne agreed. 'Head for warmer weather and some big city action, where the stolen money will buy them all the whiskey they can drink, and there are floozies aplenty to help spend what's left.'

'We've notified every town along the railroad, and will increase patrols once the snow stops. It's only a matter of time before they try and leave the country. If we can get a sighting, learn where they're going, we'll use whatever resources it takes to bring them in for trial and punishment.'

Jared said: 'We wish you luck, Lieutenant.'

'Same for the two of you. It's no picnic out there in the open, and there's a whole lot of open between here and Castle Point.'

'We'll avoid any deep ravines or canyons,' Jared said. 'They are impassable right now.'

'Let's all hope for better weather after Christmas.'

'Me and Payne will simply hope we make it to Castle Point by Christmas.'

The officer raised a hand in farewell and walked away.

'Whadda'you think?' Payne asked Jared. 'Are we gonna end up as frozen ice statues, awaiting the spring thaw, like the soldier boy says?'

'We ought to make it in two days, unless we're hit with a roaring blizzard. It's a clear sky today, so let's hope we beat the next storm.'

'Had me wondering if the train would get us this far. We was pushing a lot of snow most of the way.'

'Good thing the engine had a hefty plough on front,' Jared concurred. Then stepping back, he surveyed the string of pack animals. 'Looks like we're loaded.'

'I'm ready,' Payne said. 'But you ain't got no hair to help keep your face from freezing. You want I should cut a couple holes in a stocking cap for you?'

'The weather is going to be warm enough today. I'm hoping it isn't warm enough to melt the top layer of snow, or else we'll be busting a crust of ice with every step come tomorrow morning.'

'We've done a thorough job of wrapping our animals' legs, Valeron. That's as much as we can do.'

Jared gave a bob of his head. 'Let's get this here trek underway.'

* * *

Darcy glanced out of the front window and was rewarded by a tingle of... what was it? Warmth? Anticipation? Kinship? Or something else? Standing next to a pile of snow – recently shovelled from in front of the house – Christopher Roderick had two saddle horses waiting.

Darcy said goodbye to her mom and dad, along with Tish, her younger sister, then buttoned her coat and went out the door. As was his habit, Chris moved round to the left side of her horse to give her a leg-up. Once in the saddle, he made sure she was settled and her feet were in the stirrups before he mounted his own animal. Then they started off in the direction of Valeron.

'Sun's shining for a change,' Chris opened the conversation. 'It shouldn't be too hard to make the ride into town' – he lifted a hand to shade his eyes – 'unless we get snow blindness from the glare off the ice.'

Darcy moistened her lips, feeling the cool breeze against her face. She cleared her throat and said: 'Much preferable to our ride home Saturday night.'

'I do apologize again for not reaching town on time, Miss Valeron. My father gave me that watch on my twenty-first birthday. First time it ever stopped on me.'

'Is it working now?'

'No, I'm going to pick up another while I'm in town. If I should get to Cheyenne or Denver one of these days, I'll see if the old one can be repaired. If not, I'll save it for a

keepsake. It was the last thing my father ever gave me...'
he grinned and finished '...unless you count the four hundred head of Hereford cattle.'

Darcy took a deep breath, then quietly let it out again.
'About the other night,' she began humbly. 'I want you to
know I was angrier at the weather and getting lost than I
was with you. It's just that, well, I was really scared for a
time. I assumed Cinnamon knew the way home, but she
kept going this way and that – I'm sure she was lost, too.'

'It was still my fault. I was a half-hour late getting to
town.'

'I should have waited,' she admitted. When Chris didn't
offer anything more about it, she uttered a confession.

'In case you haven't noticed yet, I can... on a very rare
occasion... be a wee bit headstrong.' She flicked him a
cautionary sidelong glance. He held his silence, so she
continued with her confession: 'Actually, my... um... easily
aroused vexation has kept a good many men from trying
to court me.'

'Fire and ice,' Chris summed up her temper. 'That's
what Shane says about you.'

'My brother has a number of faults himself!' she was
instantly defensive.

'I'm not put off by a little spunk or a temper,
Miss Valeron,' Chris informed her in a cordial tone of
voice. 'My mom had a short fuse and the mindset of a mule
at times. I grew up thinking my father was afraid of her...
but only until I learned that Mom didn't mean anything
when she cussed one of us out. It was her personality, a part
of her make-up, and it showed how passionate she could
be about something she cared about.'

'You must miss your parents.'

'They had a good life together… almost thirty years. Dad only lasted a few months after my mother passed. He lost his zest for life.'

'I thought losing your ranch might have been what killed him.'

Chris shook his head. 'No. When Mom died, he died right along with her. He lost interest in me, in the ranch, the cattle, in most everything. He didn't have a bad heart, he had a broken heart.' His voice cracked with emotion, but he continued: 'The night my father died, we were still about fifty miles from your valley. We both knew the end had come.' He paused to swallow the sorrow, before he could finish the tale.

'When down to his final breath, Dad smiled and told me not to grieve for him. He said he was going to join my mom, and that I should be comforted by the notion that they would be waiting for me in the Great Hereafter.'

Darcy didn't realize how affected she was by his emotional tale until she discovered tears were sliding down her cheeks. Embarrassed, she blinked quickly and used the back of her mittens to wipe her face. 'This cold air!' she said hurriedly to cover her emotion. 'Every time the icy wind hits my face, my eyes begin to water!'

'I know what you mean. It's why many of the ranch hands grow beards, to counter the winter cold. I tried it once, but the itching drove me crazy. I guess a guy gets used to it, but I didn't have the patience to stick it out.'

She laughed. 'You'd look like a shaggy dog if you grew a beard.'

'What?' he kidded. 'You're not fond of shaggy dogs?'

'I sure wouldn't kiss one…' Darcy's words died in her throat as she realized what she had said. 'I mean, I…'

Thankfully, Chris laughed so as to quash her embarrassment. 'I wouldn't kiss one either, Miss Valeron.'

Casting a second gaze in his direction, Darcy regarded the young man for a long moment. 'You know, Mr Roderick,' she began hesitantly. 'As you have been my escort for the past month, I believe it would not be inappropriate for us to be on a first name basis.'

Chris didn't make a joke or laugh at the notion. Instead, he kept a sincere expression, gave a nod of approval and reciprocated: 'I'd be right honoured, so long as your folks approved.'

'I'm twenty-one years old, Christopher,' she announced. 'And I'm sure you have noticed by now, I pretty much do as I please and speak my opinion... even when no one asks for it. If I say it's all right, it's all right!'

'Fire and ice,' Chris mused, displaying his most disarming smile. 'Darcy, you're definitely fire and ice.'

***

'Injuns, you think?' Payne asked Jared, looking around the small trading post.

Jared shook his head. 'They closed the door and didn't take scalps. Two bullets in each man, both killed outright. No, this wasn't Indians.'

'Must be a dozen horses or more,' Payne remarked. 'Looks like they spent the night. Most of the hay and grain is gone.'

'You notice there isn't a bit of food, tobacco or whiskey, and the ammo is gone. Only thing left behind is an old musket and single-shot carbine.'

'Didn't want the extra weight of something useless to them,' Payne reasoned.

'A passel of horses, maybe ten or twelve men…' Jared pinned a hard look on his companion. 'This could be the bunch the army is looking for.'

Payne pointed at him to signify he was thinking along the same line. 'It makes sense. No reason to kill these two old warts, other than to ensure their silence.'

'Cold-blooded scavengers.' Jared swore softly, then put his hands on his hips. 'Can't bury anyone with the ground froze. About all we can do is wrap their bodies in something and stick them outside in their shed. We can wire the army and the US Marshal's office when we reach town.'

'That's one thing those varmints didn't take – bedding. I'll get a couple blankets for the poor souls.'

'I'll start unpacking the animals. They need to cool down before we stable them for the night. Good thing we brought our own supplies to feed them.'

The next two hours were spent tending the stock, moving the bodies of the two men from the trading post, then fixing a meal of beans, bacon and spuds. The cook stove was also used for heat, as the structure was little more than a two-room shack. It didn't feel right to sleep on the dead men's cots, so Jared and Payne tossed down ground blankets on the floor and bedded down near the fire.

After a while it was clear that both men were finding it difficult to nod off. Payne suddenly asked Jared if he had a woman in his life.

'Reckon I'll end my days on my own,' Jared replied. 'My cousin and I had it all figured out – we'd have a tidy little cabin way up Lakota Creek. We could fish right out the front door, and deer, pheasants, rabbits and ante- lope would be within walking distance for hunting. We'd visit the folks on Sundays and whenever there was a family get-together.' He let out a sigh. 'But durned if Wyatt didn't up and tie the knot with a handsome little filly a few months back.'

'Me, I've never had time to meet a respectable gal. Hauling freight here or there, gone all the time, it wouldn't be a life for a family man.'

'How did you get into your line of business?'

Payne grunted. 'I hired on to help at an express company when I was able to lift fifty pounds. Worked for my keep until I was old enough to drive. Then I joined up with an old driver and we struck out on our own. He gave the outfit and team to me when he fell ill and moved in with his brother. Once I had enough money, I bought a better team of horses and a new wagon. I've never looked back.'

'You're what – twenty-five or thereabouts?'

'Maybe a year or two older,' he said. 'My mother didn't keep track, although I been on my own since that first job.'

'Your mom doesn't sound like she had a maternal bone in her body.'

'Reckon not, and I never knew my father,' Payne related. 'Truth is, my ma didn't want me underfoot. She resented having a kid around, cause I got in the way of everything she wanted in life.'

'It's a real shame that children don't have a choice about their parents,' Jared sympathized. 'I was lucky, being born a Valeron.'

'Looking forward to meeting your brother. Bet you're proud of him, the guy being a genuine doctor and all.'

'I take it you never had any brothers or sisters?'

'Nope. My ma once told me that my being born gave her one single blessing. Seems something happened during the delivery – no idea what – but a doctor told her she could never have another child.'

Jared snorted. 'The real blessing there was for any future children.'

Payne laughed. 'You're right on target, Valeron. My being born into this world did make a difference – saved any other kid from having that woman as a mother.'

'Ought to have a much easier trip tomorrow,' Jared turned back to their current situation. 'Those men and their string of horses will have broken a trail that our animals can follow.'

'Then you figure them varmints are headed for Castle Point?'

'It's the only settlement in that direction, unless they make a sharp turn towards Laramie.'

'What are we gonna do if we catch up with them?' he asked. 'I mean, there's just you and me. Your brother's a doctor, and you said there wasn't any lawman or jail at Castle Point.'

'I'm open to suggestions, Payne. What do you think we should do?'

'Contact the army... like you said.'

'And if we get another storm? What if the army can't get to us?'

Payne grunted. 'I know you ain't thinking of us taking on a hoard of bandits by ourselves. That's six-to-one odds, and I ain't a real good shot.'

'Let's try and get some shut-eye, pard. We can worry about those desperados if we reach town and they're still there.'

'Oh, yeah,' he grumbled. 'I'm gonna sleep a whole lot better knowing we might end up on the shooting side of a dozen guns.'

'My family and I have faced greater odds before,' Jared gave him a measure of assurance. 'If it comes down to us and them, we'll send for help and pull them apart like a handful of taffy... piece by piece.'

Payne was unconvinced. 'Sure – except I never ate no taffy that was threatening to eat me first!'

CHAPTER SEVEN

Nash and Trina Valeron were having a quiet breakfast in the kitchen when the jingle of the bell at the front door announced a visitor. Before either of them could rise, Cal Woodly, the general store owner, rushed into the room. Expecting some kind of emergency, Nash began to rise so he could get his medical bag.

'No need to get up,' Cal told him, pausing to unbutton his heavy coat. 'It's not that kind of trouble... yet.'

'What's the problem, Mr Woodly?' Trina wanted to know.

'A passel of riders arrived last night,' Cal explained. 'Twelve hard-looking men, packing enough iron to start a war. They took every vacant room at the hotel and filled up the rooming house, too. They look like men on the run – not one of them with less hair on his face than a month's growth. A couple had blood on their clothes, too. Several of them are over at the café.'

'Cowhands, you think?' Nash queried. 'The blood could be from butchering an animal.'

'Joe was over at the livery – him and Denny were playing cards when the bunch come riding in. Denny had to make room for the horses, and Joe stuck around long enough to overhear how the boys plan on sticking around for a few days. They don't want to make the ride to Laramie until the sun knocks down some of the drifts. Joe said their horses were next to dead on their feet from bucking the deep snow.'

Knowing the owner of the lumber and coal business and the blacksmith, Nash didn't think either man was prone to exaggeration. He chose his words carefully.

'Tomorrow is Christmas,' he said. 'Jared was going to try and be here and spend it with us. His last wire was from Cheyenne a couple days back. If he's made decent time, he should be here sometime today.'

'I'll sure feel better with him in town,' Cal admitted. 'I gotta tell you, this crew don't look like cowboys leaving the range. They are sure enough a band of fugitives on the run.'

'Any of them look military?'

'One of them at the café was wearing soldier boots, but the others had heavy winter garb. Not a one of them has seen the wet side of a washcloth for some time. Denny said two different men seemed to be in charge, each giving orders to the others about finding rooms.'

'It doesn't seem feasible for these to be the bandits we read about in the news,' Nash speculated. 'They've been in the wind for over a month. Why would they be this close to Cheyenne after all this time?'

Cal didn't hide his apprehension. 'I don't know, Nash. Twelve men, all lookin' about as hard as railroad spikes, showing up between snowstorms? I got a bad feeling.' He shrugged. 'At least they probably won't be shopping much in my store. Other than the café, Yates is the one who has to worry most. His saloon is bound to be where they spend the bulk of their time.'

'Tell Denny and the others to keep an eye out for Jared. I told you he's bringing in as much freight as he and another guy he hired could load on a few horses. We need to warn him first thing, so he is aware of these jokers.'

'Yeah, but Jared ain't but one man,' Cal said. 'Even if he brings a hired hand, we don't have but a half-dozen men in town who know which end of a gun to shoot. These guys can take over the town if they take a mind to.'

'We can send for help, if we find they pose a threat. But let's not panic just yet. They might spend a day or two and decide the weather is good enough to head for Laramie. It'll only take a few days of clear skies and warm weather to make the trails passable again.'

'Yeah, I get what you're saying, Doc. Trouble is, we're running low on supplies. Even after Jared arrives, we'll have added fourteen more bodies to feed and house. We get another major storm and wagons can't move…'

He didn't have to finish. Nash nodded his agreement. 'Jerry's trip will have brought him through Cheyenne; he might have more information on those bandits. Could be these are just out-of-work guys travelling together, all of them going west.'

'I'll pass the word to the others about warning Jared.'

'When he contacted me with the idea in Denver, I told him to bring whatever seemed most important. I had an order or two of medical supplies, but he could have brought that with one horse. As he and the other fellow left with five or six pack animals, it should definitely help the whole town.'

'OK, so I'll get out of your way so you can finish your meal. Guess we can only wait for your brother and see how this plays out.'

'Not much choice, Cal. It's not like we can go anywhere.'

79

Darcy frowned at the store owner. 'Is this two-bit cowhand telling me the truth, Skip? Did you agree to let me off work at noon today?'

Skip grinned at her and winked at Chris. 'Tomorrow is Christmas, Darcy. You ought to get home and finish wrapping or making any presents you haven't finished yet.'

'We haven't exactly been overrun by customers lately,' she admitted. 'I must have dusted the same shelves a dozen times this week.'

'With no deliveries until the roads are open, you can go ahead and take off the day after Christmas too. I'll pay you for it – kind of a Christmas bonus.'

She smiled at her employer. 'You're an old softie, Skip. Durned if you're not.'

'You young'uns have a good time… and a merry Christmas to you both.'

Darcy went to the back room and picked up her coat, scarf and thick mittens. Chris held her coat, but then tucked the other bundle under his arm.

'First, you and I are going to have a meal at the restaurant.'

'Is this an invitation, or are you ordering me?'

He laughed. 'I've been wanting to take you on a picnic or something since we met. If you prefer, we can pick up a few items for lunch and spread a blanket on the snow. However, it's only a couple degrees above freezing, so you'll have to eat fast.'

Darcy remained unfaltering, eyeing him thoughtfully. 'Then you are *inviting* me to share a meal with you.'

'Unless you prefer to wait until you get home to eat.'

'I have some bread and Aunt Wanetta's preserves in Skip's back room for when I get hungry.'

Chris frowned in impatience. 'If you'd rather, you can bring along your bread and jam. I'm going to order myself a thick steak, fried spuds and bread pudding for dessert. You can have whatever you want, and I'll have what I want.'

Darcy allowed a mischievous simper. 'If you're going to get all huffy about it, I suppose I can let you buy me lunch.'

'Someday,' Chris sighed, 'I would like to think I'll get you to do something I ask without a fight!'

'Where would be the fun in that?'

He didn't answer, but took her by the hand. Once out on the thick carpet of snow, which had been beaten down by human traffic, he led her around the tall stacks of snow to Beulah's Café. Beulah and one of her two sisters ran the place, along with her son. Beulah was a jovial black woman who had once cooked for the Northern troops during the war. While she had never married, her sisters had wed two brothers. The family ran the café, a rooming house, and a small boot and leather shop next to the eatery. There were a couple of smaller children at home – the house shared by all of them – but the eldest boy was twelve and tended tables at the café.

'I often have the lunch special when I eat over here,' Darcy advised Chris as they entered. 'Beulah makes a chicken and dumpling dish that rivals even my mom's cooking.'

Suddenly, Beulah's nephew blocked their way. 'If you please, Miss Darcy,' he said politely. 'We have your table ready.'

Darcy stood agape, wondering what he was talking about. Chris had to tug on her arm to get her to start walking. They went through the regular dining area to a small back room. On the walls were some Christmas decorations and a neatly painted sign proclaiming 'Happy Birthday to our Lord Jesus'.

The table sported a candelabrum display with pine cones in the centre, and the table top was covered with a brightly coloured embroidered tablecloth. There were exactly two chairs, and the place setting had plates, napkins, silverware and glass goblets.

Chris moved quickly to take her coat and then hold her chair. The young waiter left without a word, as Chris removed his own coat and placed everything on a small corner table.

'What's going on?' Darcy asked in wonder. 'I didn't even know about this room!'

Before he could answer, one of the sisters brought in a small loaf of bread, still warm from the oven. She placed it on the table, along with a shallow dish of butter, then filled the glasses with wine. She giggled like a school-age girl as she left the room.

'I wanted to have a special Christmas with you, Darcy,' Chris told her softly. 'I didn't want to share it with your family or anyone else.'

'But…' was the only word she managed, before he placed a small package in front of her plate, neatly wrapped with a large red bow.

While Chris cut a slice of bread for her, she carefully removed the paper and discovered a small box. When she opened it, she gasped in awe at a silver chain with an intricately carved ivory cameo. It was the most beautiful piece of jewellery she had ever seen.

'Oh, Christopher!' she exclaimed. 'It's exquisite!'

'I tried to find something with both fire and ice,' he teased, 'but the ice kept melting.'

She laughed, removing the adornment and holding it by the silver chain. 'I can't see behind my neck to connect this – would you?'

Chris took the necklace and was ready when she lifted her hair. Draping the cameo low on her neck, he hooked the jewellery in place. He started to move back to his chair, but she caught hold of his wrist. To his surprise – and delight – she pulled him down and placed a kiss on his cheek.

He was glad he had given himself a close shave that morning, as the touch of her lips caused a warm tingle that shot through his entire body. Sitting down, he began to worry. If a simple kiss on the cheek made his knees weak, would he even survive a kiss on the lips?

***

Gauge was sitting alone in the saloon, while Lazelle and Norris were playing chequers. Four of the others were at the only other table playing cards. The rest of the men were either at the café or still in bed. All except for Elko, who had been over at the livery.

Gauge had a bad feeling about the little burg. There was no action or excitement for the men, and they had spent the last couple weeks battling the cold or boredom. He took a sip of his beer, but it didn't taste good so early in the day.

Elko entered the bar and took a moment to stand next to the pot-bellied stove in the centre of the room. He warmed his hands, then turned his backside to the heater for a few moments, before he wandered over to take a seat next to Gauge. Lazelle ambled over to join them, waiting for his report.

'If we ever get out of these one-horse towns, I'm never going to play another game of chequers!' He stared at Elko. 'Give us some good news.'

'Wind is still blowing, though not so hard,' Elko replied. 'However, the sky is clear.'

'How about the animals?' Gauge asked him.

'They are fit, but need several days before we move on. The ice crust took a lot of hide off their legs. The livery-man spent most of the night rubbing them down, treating the scrapes, and getting them warm and fed. With the barn door shut, the forge and his stove keeps a decent temperature for them.'

Lazelle swore. 'Doesn't this trash heap of a town have enough horseflesh that we can trade mounts? We need to get moving.'

'There isn't but three horses at the stable, other than ours,' Elko informed him. 'The couple of ranches nearby are snowed in and barely scrape by. Probably not a dozen horses to be had within twenty miles.'

'We'll have to sit tight,' Gauge said.

Lazelle cursed under his breath. 'Fifty cents per animal a day, along with a rubdown at two bits each. Now we're paying a dollar a day at the rooming house and about the same at the hotel for every man. Sonuvabuck! This being holed up is cutting a big slice out of our spending money.'

'What do you suggest, Laz?' Gauge snarled at him. 'You think we ought to do like you did at the trading post? Want to take over the town and kill everyone who lives here? Would that make you happy?'

'Them two might have gotten word to someone about us,' Lazelle defended his action. 'Dead men don't talk to anyone.'

'And we agreed there wouldn't be any killing unless it was absolutely necessary. It's bad enough that Braden's explosions killed and wounded several soldiers.'

84

'You gonna get a rich haul, you do what it takes, Gauge.' He narrowed his gaze. 'That's what you said about the risk before the robbery.'

'We get caught for robbery, we spend a couple years behind bars,' he argued back. 'Those men dying makes it a hanging offence.'

Instead of a rebuttal, the man averted his eyes to Elko. 'How many men have you seen around town?'

'There's a few... maybe twenty or so, but less than half are fighting age, and not many of them look capable of handling a gun. Storekeepers, hired help, a few other workers here or there. I doubt there would be more than five or six who would actually take up arms against us.'

Gauge shook his head. 'There's women and children too. It makes more sense to pay our way and not cause a ruckus. Then...' he added a pacifying option, 'we hit them the day we leave town and take it all back... plus anything they've stashed away.'

Lazelle chuckled. 'That's the first good idea you've had since the robbery.'

'I already took care of the telegraph lines to Denver and Cheyenne when we arrived in town,' Elko pointed out. 'By the time they find and repair the breaks, we'll be half-way to San Francisco.'

'Laz, tell your men to be on their best behaviour until the horses can travel. No need getting these people excited. We don't want them plotting against us.'

'I'll tell 'em,' the man went along with the idea. 'But we ain't staying one minute longer than we have to.' Then with a sour look to send a warning: 'Then we'll do whatever it takes to get back every dime we've spent. I intend to turn this town upside down and shake loose every nickle before we pull out.'

Gauge sat quietly while the heavy-set man walked back over to join Norris.

'That blowhard is gonna cause more trouble before we're shed of his company,' Elko muttered. 'I don't trust him one little bit.'

'We'll keep an eye on him… along with the rest of the men in this tiny burg.'

***

The weather held, and the top layer of snow melted down an inch or two. As had been the norm lately, during the night, the moisture formed another layer of ice, a sharp-edged crust to rake and scar the legs of animals the following day. Fortunately, Jared and Payne were able to follow the trail that the dozen or so horses had left from the same trek the previous day. It allowed them to make good time, and they made it to Castle Point by late afternoon on Christmas Eve.

Denny had expected the small caravan, so he and a couple friends had spent most of the day clearing enough snow so that he could use both the stable and the holding corral. It meant that the horses could wander about during the day, and then be housed inside at nights. So many horses filled his barn to capacity, but they would be protected from the cold.

'You chose the right day for travel, Jared!' Denny sounded off his greeting at the two men. 'Looks like you're packing a fair load of freight, too.'

Jared waved at him as he pulled his horse to a stop. 'We'll start by leaving our mounts with you, Denny. Me and my travelling partner –' he jerked a thumb at his companion – 'this is Payne – we'll go and unload the others. Payne hired on for the payment on the freight. I imagine Cal will have the invoices.'

'Yep,' the blacksmith replied. 'You're to deliver everything to him. He'll divvy it up twixt all who have something packed on your animals and tally the payment for the freight what's due.'

'Works for us.'

'You'll want to step over and talk to your brother first chance you get. We've got some concerns about some new arrivals.'

'About a dozen men, all of them armed to the teeth?'

Denny's eyes showed a glint of understanding. 'You know about 'em, do you?'

'We were able to take advantage of the trail they forged a day ahead of us. Made it much easier travel for us today.'

'They're a shady-looking bunch, skulking about like a wolf pack. Wouldn't trust them no further than I can spit.'

Jared laughed. 'I saw you hit a mouse with a stream of your chewing tobacco last time I was here.'

Denny grinned. 'Now that you bring it to mind, I don't trust them near as far as I can spit.'

'Is the telegraph working?'

'Was, when you sent us the message about the delivery of goods.' He lowered his voice and sneaked a quick look around. 'If'n it was me and I wanted to send a message, I'd do it first thing. If them fellers are up to no good, they might not want any signals going over the wire.'

'You trot over and see your brother,' Payne spoke for the first time. 'I'll lead the pack animals over to the store and help unload. Be best if you got the news of them fellers out while you can.'

'Good thinking, Payne. I'll go speak to Nash and get off a telegraph message to Fort Russell.'

'Take them a week to get organized and make the trip here... and that's if the weather holds.'

Jared agreed. 'I'll let them know what we found at the trading post and they should get troops headed this way.'

'What's the name of the store-keep?' Payne asked.

'Cal Woodly, and it's easier to unload around the back of his store... if they've cleared a path to the door. I'll be over to lend a hand, soon as I'm done at the telegraph office.'

'Should be done with all the heavy work by then,' Payne taunted. 'But that's OK. After all, you're my boss until I get paid.'

Jared hurried down the street, trying to avoid the deep snow by following the trail made by his caravan. Then he turned at the clinic, which had been recently shovelled, and entered the front door.

'Jerry!' Trina cried out a welcome. 'We saw you ride in!'

Nash also came forward to greet him with a firm handshake. 'Take your coat off and get comfortable, big brother. I'll bet you're froze right to the bone.'

'It's been a pleasant day for the trip here. I doubt it's below freezing yet.'

'Did Denny speak to you about the town's guests?'

'They are bad news, Nash. We need to contact Fort Russell right away.'

'Too late for that,' Nash told him, not hiding a deep concern. 'The line to Cheyenne and Denver went dead... about the time those guests arrived.'

Jared shrugged out of his coat and frowned. 'I noticed one of the horses we were following had left the trail for a bit and then returned. I'd wager one of the bunch cut the line.'

'We can still try Valeron. They might not be worried about the line going west.'

'Won't do much good. The troopers we need are east of here.'

'Do you think these guys are running from the law?' Trina spoke up. 'They haven't caused any trouble, and Judy said they had paid up front for the hotel rooms.'

'They killed a couple of ex-hunters that ran a trading post between here and Cheyenne. Killed them and took everything of value out of the place. Payne and I couldn't bury the bodies, except to stick them in a shed.'

'You believe they are the ones who robbed the army payroll and the Cheyenne bank,' Nash made the assumption.

'I'm sure of it,' Jared acknowledged. 'And besides the two trading-post men, the lieutenant at Fort Russell said three troopers were killed in the explosions those men set off. And a few others were injured.' Jared doubled his fists. 'These are dangerous men, and it looks like it's up to us to stop them.'

Trina did not hide her alarm at his statement. 'That's crazy, Jerry! There are twelve of them.'

'My wife makes a valid point,' Nash went along with her. 'We've only got about five men in town who could help against this bunch. None of the ranchers have come to town since the last few storms. We're cut off and on our own.'

'Have any of the gang said how long they intend to stay?'

'They have to wait a few days for their horses to heal up from the rough travel. One of them said they wanted to reach the train station at Laramie, just as soon as they could. I can't see them sticking around too long.'

'We get another major storm or two and the trains won't be able to move. The one from Denver to Cheyenne had to stop several times to clear the tracks enough to get through the snow drifts.'

'If they do leave, we would only have to get word to the army,' Trina posited. 'They would find a way to grab them down the line.

'These are a pack of murderers,' Jared said. 'I wouldn't put it past them to pillage this town before they leave. They cut off the telegraph and there are only a few men here to stop them.'

The thought put a worried look on his brother's face. 'That's a possibility, Jer.'

'OK. So if the line is open to the west, I better get a wire off to Pa and have him send us some help.'

'Better safe than suffer an attack that will ruin everyone in town,' Nash agreed, though he gave his head a woeful shake. 'Still, the help would have to get here. With all this snow, no one is getting anywhere. Those outlaws and you are the only ones to make it to our town in three or four weeks.'

'I'll send the message, if the line is still up, and we'll have to take our chances.' He tipped his head in a cocky gesture. 'If bad comes to worse, we'll do it on our own.'

'And where are you going to put a dozen killers?' Trina wanted to know.

'She's right, Jer. Even if you manage to arrest each and every one, we haven't got a jail. Everything in town that has a roof on it has animals or wood and coal stored for the winter. It would take ten men to guard them, if we had to hold them in the hotel or rooming house.'

'Denny is pretty handy at building stuff,' Jared said. 'I've an idea that might work.'

90

Nash didn't look convinced, but he knew Jared was as good as any man alive at thinking out a plan against impossible odds. 'First thing is to get a telegraph message off to Valeron,' he declared. 'They will contact the family, and hopefully send us some help.'

CHAPTER EIGHT

It was mid-morning, Christmas Day, when Elko sat down at the café's back corner table and joined Gauge, Lazelle and Hayworth for a late breakfast.

'How is it out there?' Hayworth ask. 'Can't hardly see for the snow blowing off the tops of the buildings.'

'If I hadn't brought the pair of snowshoes those old codgers kept at the trading post, I couldn't have walked a hundred feet. The crust has melted just enough that an ordinary step busts through right up to a man's knees. Even with them shoes, it took me an hour to get out of town far enough that no one would see me.'

'But you cut the wire?' Lazelle wanted assurance.

'I took it down, but it's a chore we should have done when we first arrived.'

Hayworth shrugged. 'I'm surprised to learn they even had a wire going west? There ain't nothing in that direction but Fort Bridger, and that's halfway across the state. Besides, most telegraph lines pretty much follow the rails.'

'The line that direction likely runs along one of the stage routes,' Elko offered. 'I overheard one of the locals saying the doctor is from a place called Valeron.'

'Valeron?' Lazelle repeated. 'Seems I've heard the name. Used to be a town tamer – Wyatt Valeron. Seen his name in the newspaper a time or two.'

'Webster said he knows a family that runs a café and rooming house in the town of Valeron,' Elko reported what one of the two black members of their gang had told him. 'From what little he knew about it, they have coal and lumber over that way. They probably take telegraph orders from small settlements all around. You know, there's a whole lot of open country in Wyoming. Many of the ranchers and smaller settlements need coal for heat and cooking.'

'Maybe we ought to have a conversation with whoever runs the telegraph,' Lazelle proposed. 'Could be, he sent news about us down the wire.'

'We took down the main line, the one that could hurt us,' Hayworth argued. 'Ain't gotta worry about soldiers from Fort Bridger. I doubt there's more than a handful of troopers stationed there any more. It was a big place some years back, but the fort isn't needed these days.'

'How big is this town, this Valeron?'

'A hundred people or so,' Hayworth answered Gauge. 'It's the Valeron ranch that covers a lot of the country… although I heard about a well-financed new outfit that moved in a few months back. The cattle range is overgrazed and overcrowded from here to the Mexican border. If this snow keeps up, a whole lot of cattlemen are gonna go broke.'

'What about the two freighters who arrived?' Lazelle wanted to know. 'If they came from Cheyenne, they might have gone by that trading post.'

'The one looked capable,' Elko informed them. 'The second man is a freighter by trade. I've seen him around

93

Cheyenne a time or two. He's pretty harmless. According to the blacksmith, the pair said they hit our trail about ten miles out of town.'

'Meaning they didn't ride by the trading post,' Hayworth concluded.

'Anything else we need to know about them? Gauge asked.

'The capable-looking one went to visit the medico. The guy at the livery said the two of them are related. Plus, they might have had some frostbite or something. He and the other guy spent the night at the clinic.'

'Don't know if that means anything special; there's not another bed to be had in town,' Hayworth pointed out. 'Unless the doctor gets a patient or two, he can charge rent for his extra beds.'

'We should have looked into that,' Elko said. 'Hayworth, you sometimes snore like a freight train pulling a steep grade. I might could have gotten a room of my own.

'You're almost as bad,' Hayworth retorted. 'You toss and turn like you were sleeping on a bed of hot coals!'

'How about the telegrapher?' Lazelle got back to that subject. 'I think we ought to squeeze him a little and see what pops out.'

'It would tip our hand that we're on the dodge,' Gauge reasoned. 'We don't want to give anyone the impression we're anything more than a few ex-cowpokes trying to get to Texas and warmer weather. Once the horses are ready and the sky clears, we'll clean out this coyote den and head for Laramie.'

'This waiting is gonna drive us all loco!' Lazelle complained.

Gauge pointed a finger at Elko. 'You have the Mexicans keep an eye on the two new arrivals. 'Laz, I think we ought to assign an all-night vigil – use the saloon. 'No fewer than two men on watch at all times. If we get a whiff of trouble, we've got the men and guns to take over this town.'

'We should have started out that way,' Lazelle griped. 'The widow woman who runs the laundry is pushing forty or so, but she ain't hard on the eyes. Instead of bunking alone, she could be keeping me warm at nights.'

'We don't need any extra incentive for the US marshal's office to want to track us down, Laz. Unless things go sideways, we'll do this my way. A robbery is soon forgotten, but harm a woman or child…' He didn't have to finish; the message was clear.

'Sure, Gauge,' the man accepted. 'Just giving you my opinion. No harm in that.'

Elko waved to get the attention of the elderly woman who tended tables. When she arrived, he gave his order for a meal. Soon as she walked away, Lazelle got to his feet.

'I'll talk to the boys and we'll set up a schedule for keeping an eye on this burg.'

Gauge gave an approving nod as he left the café.

'That man wants to wear your boots,' Elko told him.

'I'm thinking the same thing,' Hayworth agreed. 'With only us and the Mexicans, they have us outnumbered. I wouldn't put it past him to try something.'

'The hostility is there every time he opens his mouth,' Gauge acknowledged. 'Laz is a bull going through a corn field, trampling everything in sight. The three of us know it's better to move like a coyote and avoid disturbing the plants.'

'I should have thought to look for a telegraph wire going west. They might have gotten out a message or two.'

Gauge patted him on the shoulder. 'It's done now, Elko. We'll stay on our toes and make sure we don't have any surprises.'

'To our benefit,' Hayworth put in his own two cents, 'we know travel is brutal on horses. I doubt there'll be any wagons moving for weeks. With no forts or big towns west of here, I doubt we have any worries.'

'We'll be fine and gone if January will just bring us a couple of weeks of warm weather and sunshine.'

'That's a big *if*, Gauge. A really big if.'

***

Darcy looked at the message, then frowned at Skip. 'You say this came in on Christmas Eve?'

'Yes, but I allowed you could have Christmas and the day after off. With us being closed on Sunday...'

'Then this is three days old!'

Skip frowned. 'It's only a Merry Christmas greeting to the family. I tried to confirm whether or not it was an emergency the next morning, but couldn't get through. I suspect the wet snow brought down the line somewhere between here and there.'

'It's addressed to Uncle Locke, Skip,' Darcy pointed out meaningfully. 'He and Jared often exchange messages no one else understands.'

'Yes, but it came from Castle Point – Jared's with Nash. I can't see anything about the message that could be all that important.'

'Due to my staying in town until the weekend, Christopher won't be back for me until Saturday,' she fretted. 'If this is a crisis of some kind...' She re-read the words. It seemed a mere greeting, but with Jared...

Skip tried to absolve himself from blame. 'I showed it to Brett and he didn't think it warranted a special delivery.'

'Brett hardly ever played pinochle with the family. Wendy told me how…' she searched for the right word, '*cryptic* Jared could be.'

'Cryptic?' Skip's brows crested. 'What does that even mean?'

'In Jared's case it means that in writing he would use a secret code of some kind, innocent words that mean more than they appear.'

'All right, all right. I'll find someone to take the message,' he gave in. 'If no one is available, I'll take it myself.'

'I can do it.'

Skip held up a hand to stop her. 'No!' he declared adamantly. 'You will not! After that mishap during the storm last Saturday, I promised your folks you would stay put until Christopher arrived to accompany you home. I'm not going to have you breaking my word.'

Darcy stamped her foot. 'You all treat me like a child!'

'No, young lady,' Skip maintained. 'We treat you as we think of you: a handsome young woman who is too precious to risk losing.'

She scowled at him. 'That's unfair, using flattery to coerce me to abide by your decision!'

'Would you prefer I tie you up and leave you in the storeroom?'

'OK, I'll do as you ask, so long as someone gets the telegram to Uncle Locke – pronto!'

***

Jared lay on the cot and stared through the gloom at the ceiling. He and Payne were housed on what used to be the back porch of the clinic. Nash had helped a carpenter's daughter and the builder enclose the room with no windows, and the single door led into the examination and treatment room.

'Smells like a hospital, don't it?' he asked the freighter.

'Never been in one,' Payne replied. 'But I've smelt liniment that's 'bout the same.'

'No word back from home,' Jared said. 'Which is no surprise. The telegrapher said the line had gone dead in that direction too. Seems pretty convenient for our gang of killers.'

'You were lucky the line was still open to Valeron when we first arrived.'

'Yeah, someone overlooked that detail.' He grunted. 'But it would seem they got around to correcting the error right quick.'

'You think your family will send us some help?'

'If the message got through,' Jared answered. 'But it will take them some time to get here. If the gang's horses heal before help arrives, they might decide to leave.'

'Dunno about that,' the freighter mused. 'There's a whole lot of snow out there. You seen those fellows' horses, they've about shredded all the hide right up to their knees. Them animals won't be able to travel for another few days.'

'It's a hard trail to Laramie, if that's where they are headed. I'd wager some of the drifts are ten feet deep in spots between here and there.'

'Think we might end up doing this on our own?'

'Maybe.'

'Twelve hardened outlaws against two of us. You think that's a fair contest?'

'We could offer them a chance to recruit a few more men,' Jared joked.

'I don't much like this room. It's tight and closed in.' Payne went totally off topic. 'Sometimes my ma would stick me in a closet when she didn't want me around. If I made a sound, she would wail the daylights out of me.'

'That seems pretty harsh. How old were you when she did that?'

'Couldn't really say. It's the way it was for as far back as I remember.'

'And you left home at twelve or so?'

'It was actually a year or two sooner. I was fair sized for my age. I think I was about ten when I hired out and left home.'

'She allowed you to start working at a real job?'

'Glad to be rid of me.'

'That's rough, Payne. Did you ever see her again?'

He heaved a sigh. 'No need. I heard she'd been strangled to death.'

Jared sat up straight. 'When did this happen?'

'I reckon it was three or four years ago. I don't keep track of time very well.'

'That's a strange coincidence.'

'What do you mean, a coincidence?'

'I happened to take on the task of trying to find a man who has strangled several women… all of them ladies of the evening, parlour-type gals.'

'Yep, I heard some talk about that when I was in Denver. I kind of figured it must be a travelling salesman, or maybe a drifter who had a grudge against women.'

'And you don't remember your father?'

'Gone before I was old enough to know him. Ma said he died in the war.' He grunted, as if in disbelief. 'Truth is, Ma had a fair number of male friends. It's why she used to stick me in the closet. It's the reason this room makes me nervous.'

Jared reclined once more. 'Well, I'll continue the search for that crazy cuss come spring. First off, we have to deal with these outlaws.'

'What about us waiting to see if these bandits ride out? Maybe they won't start no trouble?'

'The storekeeper says they are spending a lot of money. My guess is, it's because they figure to rob every store in town when they leave. The telegraph wire being down in both directions is a little too convenient.'

'Yeah, and it strikes me odd, it happened about the time we arrived. You think them boys suspect we found those two dead men at the trading post?'

'I told Denny to tell anyone who asked that we didn't hit the trail of those fellows until we were about ten miles from town. If they believe that story, we shouldn't have to worry. After all, going to the trading post was a couple miles out of our way.'

'Glad you was thinking ahead, Valeron. Do we sit and wait for your kin?'

'I've no hold on you, Payne. Soon as you think your animals are ready, you can take your money and ride. It's been clear the last few days. You could probably make it to Cheyenne on your own.'

'I was at the trading post when we found those dead ex-trappers,' the man expressed his anger. 'I'll be here when you arrest their killers!'

'You're a good man, Payne.'

He harrumphed. 'I ain't all that good, but them boys got to pay for their crimes.'

***

Locke had summoned the family and a few of the other men to a meeting. It was late afternoon before everyone arrived. Temple and Udall conferred with their older brother, the undisputed patriarch of the Valeron family. Others in the main room included Shane, Landau, Cliff, Sketcher and Christopher, along with the two Lakota Indians and several ranch hands.

After a short discussion amongst the three elder states-
men, Locke uttered an 'ahem!' and the room grew deadly
silent.

'I'm sure all of you heard about the brazen robberies
at Fort Russell and the Cheyenne bank. Several troopers
were killed or injured by several explosions, while the ruth-
less bandits got away with the army payroll and emptied
out the bank. It was determined there were no less than a
dozen men involved.' He paused, glancing over the group
to make sure that no one had a question. Obviously, they
had all learned those details.

'Jared sent a wire from Castle Point. To protect the
telegrapher or anyone else from knowing what the message meant, he fashioned it as a Christmas greeting. In it,
he says to remember the twelve days of Christmas when we
think of him. He also wrote how he wished we could be
there, seeing as how he couldn't be here with us… and he
was going to miss the exchange of presents.'

Locke allowed the words to sink in. 'Jared has not
exchanged presents with anyone in the family in a decade.
And we have never done anything special concerning the
twelve days before Christmas. Plus, the boy who delivered
the message said the telegraph line went dead the day after
Jared arrived at Castle Point. If he hadn't sent a wire right
off, it wouldn't have reached us at all.'

'Twelve days – twelve bandits,' Shane interpreted. 'And
he wishes we were there to exchange presents.' He heaved
a sigh. 'Means he is going to try and arrest those twelve
men himself, unless we send him help.'

'Boy o' Friday!' Cliff exclaimed. 'Jerry is about as
good as a man can get, but to take on a dozen killers? By
himself?'

'We can't let him try it alone,' Locke countered. 'We're
going to send him whatever help we can.'

'How do we get there?' Chris wanted to know. 'It's all Miss Darcy and I can do to make it to and from Valeron, and that's keeping the trail open by travelling it every week. It takes about three to four hours if the weather is good. We can't move the horses any faster or they'll cut their legs to pieces.'

'It's a full day's ride by stage to reach Castle Point from town,' Cliff pointed out. 'If a man gets caught in a blizzard…?'

'It's a risk,' Locke admitted. 'And I'm not sure going by horse is the best way to travel.'

'If you're talking snowshoes,' Shane jumped in, 'we'd be two days and nights getting there.'

Chris threw in his experience: 'It's tough going, but I've been forced to camp a time or two up in Montana during a storm. It would mean packing shelters and extra blankets, but it can be done.'

'There's the way station at Rabbit Ears,' Shane recalled. 'The stage changes horses there. If we could make it that far, we could stay the night with the old hermit that runs the place.'

'Good thinking, Shane,' Cliff said. 'The only drawback is that we would have to follow the stage route so we don't miss it. You know, the road goes down to the Little Lakota stream, so they can water the team. Plus, the way station is several miles short of being half way between Valeron and Castle Point.'

'OK,' Temple was the one to speak. 'You can ride horses to Valeron and spend the night. The next morning, if the snow is too difficult for the horses, you can leave on foot with snowshoes. With decent weather, you can make Castle Point from Valeron in two days.'

'That's a good timetable, but only if we don't get hit with another storm,' Sketcher reminded them. 'A ground blizzard – out there in the open – with temperatures well below zero?' He shook his head. 'It's a big risk.'

'That's why no married men are going, Sketcher,' Locke told him.

'I'm not married… yet,' Cliff retorted.

'You're still on the gimpy side from your last adventure with Jared,' Reese pointed out.

Before the debate could get started, Locke raised his hands to quiet the room. 'Shane, you and Christopher will lead the party. Takoda and Chayton will go along as guides, too. As for anyone else, we'll only send another couple volunteers.'

'Need to keep the number down, in case things don't work out,' Chris suggested. 'The more men, the more chance we'll lose someone if the weather turns bad.'

'Me and Johnson will go,' Amos spoke up. 'It will give Jared six guns, and I reckon he and Nash will have a few men lined up. Six of us ought to be enough to tip the scales in our favour.'

'You're sure Johnson will agree?' Temple asked him. 'I mean, he's still out with the cattle.'

'Him and me consider ourselves to be family members,' Amos stated. 'We followed trail drives year after year until you hired us on. None of the other cattle owners ever treated us like anything other than a hired hand. You people here… you have shared your holidays and birthdays with us, treated us like good friends instead of a couple stray cowpokes, which is what we were. Nope, him and me will be making this trip. No argument or discussion is needed.'

Locke chuckled. 'Amos, you make me feel cheap for only giving you and Johnson a twenty dollar Christmas bonus.'

'So when can everyone be ready to ride?' Takoda asked.

'Pack up what you'll need,' Locke remained in charge. 'Make sure you have good snowshoes and the warmest gear you own. If you need anything extra, contact one of us here at the house. Barring a raging storm, everyone be ready to leave at first light.'

'Breakfast will be served at six in the morning,' Udall offered. 'Faye and I will prepare a good meal for you six men.'

The room was suddenly filled with serious discussion, the men comparing gear, thinking ahead about warm gloves, ear protection, boots and snowshoes. Everyone in the room offered to help the six volunteers gather the belongings they would need. This was a dangerous rescue mission, and there was a good chance some of the men going would not return.

CHAPTER NINE

It was well after dark and getting late. Jared was thirty feet down the alleyway between the saloon and the general store, burrowed in a hole next to the window of the main bar-room, a single wall away from where the man called Gauge was sitting. Half covered in snow, Jared had his poncho wrapped around his body to keep the snow from melting into his clothes. He had about given up on hearing anything worthwhile when a second man joined the gang leader.

'Sitting alone, Gauge?' the new arrival asked the obvious question.

'Have a seat, Elko,' came the response. 'Lazelle is playing cards with a couple of his men over in his room. He's about as nervous as a young mare seeing a stallion for the first time.'

'I know it's on your mind, chief,' the half breed said quietly. 'But that man ain't got one grain of loyalty for anyone but himself. I don't trust him no more'n a rabid dog.'

'We wanted to pull both jobs at once,' Gauge argued. 'It was either throw in with him or skip the bank.'

'I know why he's with us, but I can't shed the bad feeling about him. I'm convinced he intends to double-cross us first chance he gets.'

'I'm a step ahead of him, my friend. He thinks Braden is on his side, but I had a private talk with him a short while back. I promised to triple his share, if he keeps an eye on Lazelle and informs us of any planned trickery.'

'You think he's trustworthy?' Elko then added: 'What if Lazelle sniffs out that his loyalty is shaky and makes him a better offer?'

Gauge dismissed his concern. 'Hayworth and the Mexicans are with us. So long as we keep Braden on our side, or even neutral, that makes the odds even – six and six. Lazelle won't try anything without having the ratio in his favour.'

'You're the man with the plan,' Elko confirmed. 'If you get me killed, I reckon it's my fault for sticking with you all this time.'

Gauge laughed. 'If we both end up dead, it won't matter who's to blame.'

'I did some scouting this morning,' Elko turned to business. 'Slipped out of town without anyone being the wiser and checked the telegraph lines – both directions. No one has tried to fix them. I didn't see a single track in the snow where anyone had been out there looking for the break.'

'It was good thinking to down the lines a mile from town. I doubt anyone will even try to find the breaks until the snow melts down a foot or two.'

'The wind is picking up, coming in from the north again. If we get another storm, it's going to be a cold one.'

'We can't make a move until we're certain we can make it to Laramie.'

Elko bobbed his head. 'It's January now, and that's never a good month in this part of the country. Wish we could have left on Christmas Day. We've had several good days in a row. I'm afraid it won't last.'

'We didn't know what the weather would do, and the animals had to recover so they were in good enough shape to travel.' Gauge displayed his underlying concern. 'I hate to delay much longer. This sitting around is wearing on every one of the men.'

'There's been a couple of near fights,' Elko said. 'We need to get moving.'

'I looked at the horses this morning while you were checking the wire. Their legs have pretty much healed. I think we can leave in the next day or two… if the weather cooperates.'

'We'll also follow the lead of those two freighters and wrap hides around each of the horse's legs to protect them. Their animals arrived in pretty good shape.'

Gauge flashed a smirk. 'When we leave, we'll take the teamster's draft horses to break trail for us until they give out. It will save our horseflesh for the remainder of the trip.'

'The freighter might have something to say about that.'

'I don't care for their looks, Elko. They've been friendly to most every man in town, yet never said a word to any of us. They might be trouble.'

'Tell it to Lazelle,' Elko advised. 'He will be happy to eliminate any threat they might present.'

Gauge uttered a sigh of resignation. 'I'm afraid we were thinking too big this time. I didn't want any murders on our heads.'

'Can't look back, once you've crossed that line,' his friend said. 'Men are dead and we're responsible. That seals our fate.'

'OK, it's nothing we can change now. We'll deal with them when the time comes to depart this burg and clean out every business in town.'

'When do you think – Sunday?'

'If we don't get another storm,' Gauge went along with the time schedule. 'That would work to our advantage, and maybe save some lives, too. If we catch everyone at the church meeting, we'll take over the room. A couple of men can keep watch over the congregation. We'll fleece them one by one, then clean out their homes and shops. When we leave, we'll take every horse with us for the first coupla miles. That way, no one is going to catch up with us from behind.'

'Want to tell Laz, so he'll have his men ready?'

'Not until Saturday night, and only if the sky is clear. That joker's too blasted anxious as it is. We don't want him having time to think up a way to doublecross us and leave us behind.'

***

Jared made his way down to the blacksmith shop and warmed himself by the stove. He took a quick inventory and saw Denny had a buckboard, a one-horse buggy and a sorry-looking prairie schooner that was covered in a foot of snow. After considering what there was to work with, he explained what he had in mind to the blacksmith.

Denny questioned him about details and went through his stock of iron, bolts and chains. Having visualized the chore Jared had in mind, he said, 'If I need anything, Joe likely has it on hand. He always stocks up after our summer business. Betwixt him and me, we'll get the job done.'

'OK, but you'll need to do the work on the sly, so none of the gang gets suspicious.'

'Fixing up that old wagon makes sense. One of them asks 'bout it, I'll say it's so I can sell it to the next pilgrim family that comes along wanting to upgrade from a hand-cart. Won't be any reason for anybody to think otherwise.'

'We need to be ready by Saturday night.'

'You kin put your trust in me, Jared. I'll get the job finished in time.'

Jared bid him goodnight and left the man to get started.

Although Nash and Trina had already gone to bed, Payne was sitting on his bunk, awake and waiting to hear what Jared had learned.

'You are made of hearty stock,' Payne opened the conversation. 'Bet it's not more than 20 degrees out there right now. And there you was, burrowed into an icy hole like a badger.'

'It was cold, but worth it,' Jared told him. He explained what he had overheard, and ended with, 'It doesn't leave us a lot of time.'

'You think your family will get here before then?'

'With the fair weather we've been having, I thought they might have been here before now. If they don't show, we'll be on our own.'

'I know Nash plans to help some, along with a couple of the men in town. Even so, do you really think we can take down that many men?'

'Once we start, there won't be any turning back.' He grinned. 'As an added incentive, you recall me telling you that their boss man – the one called Gauge – thinks you and I would be trouble. If we don't attend the Sunday meeting, he intends to kill us both right off, ransack the town and take your team.'

'Now I ponder it, I reckon I won't sneak out of town and leave you all by your lonesome,' Payne joshed. 'Killing me is one thing, but stealing my team…' He snorted. 'That's enough to provoke a nun into taking up arms.'

'We've got a couple days. We need to get an idea of each member of the gang, where they'll be and what they'll be doing. It's the only way we can determine how to pick these guys off a couple at a time. How are you fixed for weapons?'

'Well, I've got a hunting knife in my knapsack, along with a box of shells for my rifle or handgun – both use the same bullets. That's about it for me.'

'I wish we had a shotgun for you,' Jared said. 'You did say you weren't much of a shot.'

'I ain't never shot myself, so my advice to you is to stay behind me if it comes to gun play. If nothing else, I'll be good cover for you.'

Jared chuckled. 'If my idea works out, we might not have to fire a shot. Still, I'd feel a whole lot better if some of the people from my ranch got here before we have to act.'

***

Darcy and Brett were at the Valeron jail when the six men arrived from the ranch. While Brett spoke with Shane and the others, she dragged Chris a few steps away.

'Tomorrow is Saturday,' she said tersely. 'Am I supposed to ride home alone on the trip to the ranch?'

'Your pa said he would send Faro in to collect you.'

Darcy turned her back on him. 'I can't believe you are risking your life like this. You are a partner, not one of the hired hands!'

'It's for Jared's sake,' Chris reminded her. 'There are twelve killers! He has to have help!'

'Brett is a lawman! Wyatt is the fastest man with a gun in the country! You're no gunman. Let the professionals go and help Jared.'

Chris reached out and placed a hand on her shoulder. She shook it off.

'Those men are married, Darcy. They have wives, and Brett has a child.'

'I know all that!' she snapped. 'It's just that… that…'

110

Chris rested a consoling hand on her shoulder a second time and forcibly turned the girl around so he could see her face. He didn't fully understand her anger... until he saw she had tears in her eyes.

'Dad-blame, Darcy!' he exclaimed. 'Why didn't you tell me? Why have you kept your feelings hidden?'

'What are you talking about?' she fumed.

'You've got feelings for me!' The words came out more triumphant and louder than he had intended. 'I mean,' he hurried to lower his voice. 'I'm crazy about you – you had to have seen it. My heart was yours from the first time I looked into your eyes.'

'Will you stop!' she demanded in a hushed voice. 'This isn't the time for...'

'The heck it isn't!' he cut her off. 'If I should get myself killed on this trip, I would die a much happier man if you were to let me kiss you once.'

Rather than risk her brother and the others overhearing any more than they already had, she took hold of Chris by his wrist and led him to the rear of the office, to the two jail cells. Without a word she dragged him into the small cubicle and closed the door. He stood bewildered, until she threw her arms around him and kissed him... hard.

Chris couldn't breathe, couldn't think, couldn't move from within her embrace. When she broke contact and stepped back, he could barely remain standing.

'There!' she declared, visually out of breath too. 'I've kissed you. Now, will you reconsider going on this stupid trip?'

Chris had to swallow an overwhelming passion that threatened to consume his very being. 'Darcy...' His shoulders sagged under the weight of the words he had to say.

'I already gave my word. Jared and Nash need help. The people in the town of Castle Point could be hostages of these men already.'

'But,' her loving gaze melted his resolve, 'I'm confessing to you, Christopher – I'm admitting I love you.'

He took her in his arms and kissed her a second time. As he held her close, he put his lips up next to her ear and whispered a few tender words. After holding her for a short time, he confirmed his intentions.

'I'm used to Montana winters, Darcy,' he explained gently. 'I have an uncanny ability to always know where I am. There are storm clouds off to the north. If we get hit by a major storm, I might be the only one that can lead Shane and the others to safety.'

Pushing him back, Darcy shook her head. 'I saw the Indians are with you. Takoda and Chayton have lived in this land all their lives. They don't need *you* to tell them where they are.'

'No one else could have gotten you home when you got lost in that last big storm. No one else would have even found you – Takoda included. I've got to see these men safely to Castle Point. After that, I'll do as Jared tells me. Shane told me Jared has never gotten one of the men with him killed.'

'Both Shane and Jared came awfully close the last time. Jared's life was saved by a girl!'

He smiled at her concern. 'You know I have to do this, Darcy. It breaks my heart to leave you, but I intend to be a part of this family. I have to do my share to earn that position.'

'You only have to stay alive and ask me to marry you!' she flared. 'Shane and the others won't fault you for staying here. They know I can be a tyrant when I'm pushed.'

'I love you for worrying about me, my dearest Darcy, but I can't back out at the last minute.' When she ducked her head to hide the tears of disappointment, he murmured: 'I promise you... I will return, just as soon as I can. I swear it on my love for you.'

Darcy came back into his arms, resting her chin against his shoulders. 'If you break your promise, I'll hound your ghost through eternity.'

'That's a threat I will take very seriously, my love. Believe me... I'm coming back.'

***

Saturday morning brought gales of wind that shook the buildings. Then the snow flurry increased to a snow fury. By noon the vicious storm was a lethal, roaring blizzard. Raw, icy gusts rocked the earth, mixed in with a blinding sheet of ice crystals. They struck like pellets from a shotgun barrel, forming an impenetrable wall that enveloped and devastated everything in its path. The swirling of the wind lifted the granular sleet from the ground, while the assault of new beads of frozen snow caused a swirling action, engulfing everything in its path like a raging tornado.

Jared and Payne crossed the street to reach the general store. It took most of their strength and several minutes to manage the hundred feet. Cal opened the door for them and had to have help to close it again.

'Holy Hannah!' Jared asserted. 'We've got a hog-wild, rip-roaring Wyoming blizzard on our hands. The wind must be gusting at seventy or eighty miles per hour. If this lasts for more than a day or two, it'll wipe out half the herds of cattle throughout the entire country.'

'Don't remember ever running into a storm as bad as this,' Payne agreed. 'And I've been a teamster for fifteen years.'

Cal looked around the store, although he knew it was empty of customers. His wife was at the house with the kids. 'I don't think we need worry about any action tomorrow,' he spoke under his breath to Jared. 'These bandits aren't going to light out for Laramie in this.'

'It might depend on how long the storm lasts,' Payne commented. 'There's a chance it'll blow itself out this afternoon.'

'A blizzard coming in this hard?' Cal looked again out of the window – it was a blank, white curtain. 'These sometimes last for days. Plus, it could put down another foot of snow, and that powerful wind will make for some catastrophic drifts.'

Jared gave him and Payne a thoughtful look. 'If the weather doesn't let up by tomorrow, it might be a good time for us to take action.'

'Wait a minute!' Cal was shocked at the idea. 'I just said those men won't try anything in the middle of a blizzard.'

'Yes,' Jared acknowledged, 'and they won't be expecting us to try anything, either. We could take them by surprise.'

'Surprise?' He snickered at the idea. 'There are twelve of them – half in the boarding house, three rooms with two men each, and half at the hotel, taking up four rooms. Ever since you arrived, several of them stay up all night at the saloon. How on earth do we surprise that many men, who are obviously on guard, and living in that many different rooms?'

'I'm working on it,' Jared assured him.

'Even if we could grab up every one of them, what do we do with them?' Cal voiced his uncertainty. 'We'd still be forced to house and feed them, same as we are now – ' his dagger-like stare bored into Jared, 'unless you intend to hang them all without a trial?'

Jared returned a stern look on the storekeeper. 'These guys murdered the two men at a trading post twenty miles from here; they killed and wounded a number of troopers at Fort Russell; and they robbed the bank at Cheyenne. Add to that, I overheard them planning to strip this town bare when they leave. We can't sit back and wait for them to act. By then it'll be too late.'

Cal took a deep breath and let out a sigh of submission. 'You're right, Jared, every blessed word. It's just the notion of so few of us taking on so many of them… it scares the hell out of me!' He gave another sigh, this time of resignation. 'Tell me what you want from me.' He shook his head. 'Then tell me where the devil we're going to put them?'

'First off, we can't be seen gathering together. If they get suspicious, we're done,' Jared warned. 'Me and Payne have worked out a few ideas. We'll put everything in order and tell each man what he needs to do. If the blizzard doesn't blow itself out by morning, we'll put the plan into action tomorrow night.'

'How many have offered to join with us?' Cal asked.

'There's us three, along with Joe and Tolkin – he's been helping Yates at the saloon. Yates wants to throw in, but he's pushing seventy and doesn't get around very good. Other than that, we've only got Nash.'

'What about Denny?'

'Denny's already on the job. He was the first to sign on.'

'Well, I know you aren't gonna risk Nash's life, and Tolkin has four kids. Besides that, I'm a family man too. How much help can any of us be without getting ourselves shot full of holes?'

Jared lifted his hand in a sign of reassurance. 'Me and Payne will handle the gang. We only need a little help from the rest of you to make everything work.'

'A little help?' Cal laughed, though it lacked any humour. 'I'd prefer a company of soldiers and about twenty extra lawmen.'

Jared grinned. 'Where would be the challenge in that?'

CHAPTER TEN

As one, the small group of men staggered to a halt. To inhale too deeply was to feel ice coating the lungs, while stopping for more than a minute or two was to freeze and be buried alive. All six formed a circle, huddled shoulder to shoulder to form a wind block.

'Bad choice leaving before daylight,' Shane shouted to Chris over the roar of the storm. 'Otherwise we'd have woke up to this and stayed in our blankets.'

'I've never seen it any worse than the last few hours,' Chris informed him. 'And we had some dandy storms in Montana.'

'We should have turned back when the wind picked up. Most of this snow isn't falling from the sky, it's blowing back and forth. It's one of those sideways ground blizzards.'

Takoda put his hand on Shane's shoulder to get his attention. 'When the god of wind paused to take another breath, I was able to see Eagle's Nest. It's north of us. The way station is at least ten miles southeast of here.'

'We sure haven't made much distance,' Shane lamented. 'Near as I can tell, we've been walking steadily uphill and mostly in circles. If you can see Eagle's Nest, we're not even half way to Rabbit Ears.'

Chris removed the glove from one hand, dug out his timepiece and looked at it. 'It's already noon,' he called out to the others. We can't possibly make that far before dark.'

'I agree,' Takoda said. 'The wind has knocked me off my feet several times. We are barely moving forward.'

'It's a waste of time and our energy to continue,' Chris determined. 'I reckon it took a half hour to go the last hundred yards… and it's getting worse. With this bitter cold and wind, I doubt we'd all survive a night out in this.'

'No way could we put up a tent for shelter,' Shane said. 'We're down to a crawl to keep from being blown away. Pull out a piece of canvas and it would likely fly a man into the next state.'

'Having seen a landmark, what's our exact position?' Chris asked Takoda.

The Lakota Indian pointed off to the north. 'Eagle Nest is there.' Then he knelt in the snow, sheltered by the men huddled around him. Chris hunkered down so he could make out Takoda's rough drawing of a map in the snow. He marked the approximate location of the landmark, then estimated the location of the Rabbit Ears way station. Lastly, he made an 'X' showing both Castle Point and Valeron, from whence they had started. It allowed Chris a clear determination of their position.

'Good,' he said, studying the rough graphics. 'It looks like we've kept a fairly straight line. That will make it easier to find our way back.'

'Then we're giving up?' Shane wanted to confirm.

'Six dead men will not help Jared one bit,' Chris told him. 'If we turn back now, we might make Valeron by dark.'

'Yes, but it's going to be hard to keep moving in the right direction,' Takoda warned. 'There are no landmarks on the return trip.'

Chris outlined: 'Against this wind, we'll have to form a chain. If one of us becomes lost, it would mean certain death.'

'How do we make a chain?' Takoda inquired.

'You and I will each lead two men. Get a piece of rope and have them tie it around their waists. You take Shane and Chayton and I'll take Amos and Johnson. That way, if we get separated, you and I have the best chance of leading the way home.'

'Takoda and Chayton are getting a little old for this,' Shane complained. 'I might have to carry them both, in order to reach town.'

'We've been carrying you since you were a child,' Takoda teased. 'It's time you paid us back.'

Chris looked again at his new pocket watch. 'We've at most five hours of daylight left. We'll have to work twice as hard on the return, due to the wind being in our face.'

'I can't tell which way the wind is blowing,' Shane groaned. 'It seems to be coming from every direction at once.'

'Get a line around yourselves, and I'll hook up my pair. We don't have a minute to spare. When it gets dark, the temperature will sink like a rock in a pond.'

'You fellows quit spooning the sugar and get to the mush,' Amos quipped by way of rejoinder. 'Me and Johnson are looking more like snowmen every second. We want to sleep in a warm bed tonight. Can't do that if we keep jawing out here.'

'Wrap the rope around yourselves and start walking,' Takoda told Amos. 'We'll be right behind you.' He offered a frosty grin. 'You can be our windbreak.'

***

'It's raising holy hell out there,' Lazelle griped to Gauge, as he sat down across the bar-room table from him. 'Can't see a foot in any direction – worse than a moonless night at the bottom of a well.'

'It looks like we'll be here a while longer,' Gauge concurred unhappily. 'As for the train, even if they clear the tracks enough to keep the locomotive running west, they'll be bogged down with this storm. They won't be sticking to any timetable.'

'Bet the drifts are ten feet high in the low places. As for the mountains…' Lazelle grunted wryly. 'We sure can't get far, not with every ravine and coulee stacked up with twenty feet of snow and glazed over with ice. One wrong turn and we'd be stuck in snow over our heads.'

'Good thing those two teamsters got through with those supplies. Otherwise we'd have been starving right long with the locals.'

'That's about the only positive thing about sitting in this rabbit hole.'

'Have you or your men heard or seen anything we should be worried about?' Gauge wanted to know. 'Anyone been asking questions or acting suspicious?'

'No, but that in itself is a something to worry about. We're eating and drinking more than most of the locals, yet not one of them has asked when we intend to leave.'

'Could be, word has gotten around about our horses needing time to heal. Or, it might be the cash we brought in, Laz. These folks are probably used to making all of their money during the good weather months. This little windfall is likely making it easier for them to get through the winter.'

'Always looking at the up side of things, ain't you Gauge?'

'I keep a gun handy and ears open all the same,' was his reply. 'Hope for the best, be ready for the worst. It's a philosophy you ought to try sometime.'

Laz showed a sneer. 'I only use that philosophy on women.'

'How are your boys holding up?'

'Like they sat down in the dark and realized they had squatted on a red ant hill.' He threw up his hands. 'Why the hell did we have to pick a town where they turn off the lamps at eight 'o clock every night, and don't have one blessed dance-hall girl?'

'It's a crossroad settlement,' Gauge pointed out. 'Mostly pilgrims that can't afford the train, and a few travellers. Even the cow herds don't come near this place.'

'I've only seen one pretty woman in town… and she's married to the doctor.'

Gauge clicked his tongue. 'Yeah, can't mess with her. Never know when one of us might need a medico.'

'Rogers and Norris are having a poker game in their room. You want to sit in?'

'Norris is a little too good with cards. I'd sooner save my share of the money for the gambling tables and pretty girls at San Francisco.'

'Fine.' Lazelle didn't seem surprised. 'I'll see you tomorrow.'

'If we aren't all buried alive during the night.'

'Yeah, that's actually a possibility.'

***

Skip came in from shovelling the walkway in front of the store. He shook himself out of his coat and knocked the inch of crusted snow from the garment.

'Waste of time,' he grumbled to Darcy. 'I can't shovel as fast as it covers the walk. Besides which, I can't even see the buildings across the street. We're locked up in one direful storm.'

'Shane and the others shouldn't have left town this morning.' Regret was thick in her voice. 'How can anyone see where they are going in that stuff?'

'I don't know,' Skip admitted. 'I doubt I could get to the livery without getting lost. You can't open your eyes enough to see where you're going. It's a blinding wind-storm, because the hard bits of snow hit like grains of sand. I've been hoping against logic to see the boys returning home.'

'But they won't,' Darcy did not hide her fears. 'Shane has always answered the call when Jared beckoned. Ever since we were little, Shane worshiped him. Jared did that or this; he's the best tracker in the country; he's the best shot with a rifle… My brother has always looked at Jared as if our cousin was his own personal hero.'

'I remember your father and Locke talking about it one time,' Skip told her. 'Temple was complaining to your uncle that Shane was more his son than one of your family's.'

Darcy moved over to the window. It was glazed over with ice and snow until there was only a spot or two where she could look out.

'Can anyone survive a storm like this, Skip? Do you think they can make it to Rabbit Ears?'

'Takoda and Chayton lived on the plains for many a year with their tribe, then as scouts for the army. And Shane told me no one else but Roderick could have found you the night you were lost. He said that guy's sense of direction was beyond anyone he had ever met.'

Darcy grimaced as the wind rattled the doors and seemed ready to lift the roof. How did anyone stand against Nature? Hurricanes, tornadoes, earthquakes, floods, blizzards? Rather than consider the odds against

Chris and the others, she closed her eyes and murmured a prayer for their safety.

***

Jared looked over Denny's handiwork and gave his approval. 'It's exactly what we need. Make sure it's as solid as possible. One weak point, one missed spot, and it might mean the death of us all.'

'One thing in our favour,' Denny said. 'That fellow, Elko, is the only man who has been to visit lately, and his concern is the horses. The animals are healed up and ready, but no one is going to try leaving town with this unholy storm going on. I must have shovelled for an hour to reach the water trough. And if I didn't have a pump house to protect it, there wouldn't be drop of water available for the animals. I'd be melting snow at the forge.'

'Having that small stove at the pump house is one of the smartest set-ups I've ever seen. I'm going to tell my father about it. We have a small heating unit for the barn, so we can keep a sick or baby animal warm, but no one ever gave a thought to building a structure over one of the pumps. Come winter, we either haul the water or melt it to save in water barrels.'

'Be cold inside the wagon,' Denny warned him. 'I reckon you'll need a lot of blankets and such.'

'Not something I'm worried about. My first concern is how to arrest all of them without getting anyone killed.'

'Are you sure you won't need me to help in other ways? I'm not much of a hand with a gun, but I can help cart a body off if necessary.'

'You're in for a full share of the responsibility, Denny. It will be us providing you with extra help once it's over.'

'You mean, if we ain't all shot full of holes or lying out in the storm dying.'

Jared chuckled. 'You sound like one of my brothers or cousins. They aren't always eager to go along with my schemes.'

'Only thing positive I can say about that is they're all still alive and kickin'. If I can say the same when this is done, I'll be a happy man.'

'You're sure no one has taken notice of your handi-work?' Jared did a last check.

'Nope. I've done most of the work at nights or early in the morning. I been trying to keep most everything look-ing normal.'

'It would have fooled me,' Jared agreed. 'Let's hope it can do the job.'

'I just hope you've come up with a good enough plan for this to work.'

'Me too, Denny,' Jared said. 'I'll see you later.'

***

Darcy insisted on keeping the lights on inside the store, even after Skip had gone to bed. She didn't dare sleep, worried about Christopher, her brother, and the other men who had risked their lives to brave such a terrible storm.

The wind continued to howl like a pack of voracious wolves terrorizing a weak or crippled animal and desperate for a meal. She spent her time sitting next to the pot-bellied stove, adding a chunk of coal now and again when it began to cool. Skip would have scolded her about wasting their precious store of coal, but she wanted the place warm... in case several near-frozen men should come staggering in from the raging storm.

She began to pace, unable to sit still for more than a few minutes. How her heart ached when she thought of people she loved being out on such a night. If only she could be certain they had made it to the way station, she could have gone to bed and….

Something heavy thudded against the front door! Darcy thought it must have been an overhang of snow falling from the roof. But then the door was pushed open!

Shane was first through it, followed by the other five men, all coated in a heavy layer of ice and snow. With them being so heavily bundled up, the only thing showing was their eyes.

'Sis!' Shane managed a muffled word through the thick woollen scarf wrapped about his face. 'Thank heavens you have a fire going!'

The last man closed the door and then everyone started to work their frozen fingers to remove their encrusted overcoats, gloves and headgear.

Darcy hurried over to lend a hand, shouting at Skip to get up. He groggily entered the room in his nightshirt, robe and slippers.

'Get some coffee on!' she ordered. 'We've got to thaw these men out.'

'Comin' right up!' he replied, instantly awake from the excitement. 'The pot is ready. I'll stick it on the stove to heat.'

As each man became free of their frozen outer wear, they huddled around the stove and began trying to remove their foot gear. It was rather clumsy, considering they still wore the snowshoes. The rawhide straps were frozen so Chris and Takoda used their knives to cut the men's boots free. Then the boots themselves were removed so the men could thaw their nearly frozen feet.

'Good thing you had the store lights on,' Chris told her. 'We nearly missed the town. With the wind and snow… it was black as the inside of a stove pipe. I saw the flicker of light from the store windows and knew we'd made it.'

'You shouldn't have left until you could see the sky,' Darcy criticized their eagerness to leave that morning. 'It's a wonder you got back at all.'

'No argument from us,' he agreed. 'But the blizzard didn't hit until we were a couple miles out of town. We kept hoping it would let up long enough to make the way station, but it kept getting worse.'

'And worse!' Shane added. 'I'm telling you, sis, we were about five minutes from dying out there.' He pointed at Chris. 'If this bloodhound hadn't kept us marching in the right direction, none of us would have made it.'

Chris laughed. 'I was following my heart, future brother-in-law.'

Darcy sucked in her breath at his statement. She couldn't stop the rush of blood that coloured her cheeks. When Shane gave her a questioning look, she bulled her way forwards. 'You men! Get to warming the life back into those frozen fingers and toes before I have to take a sharp knife and start cutting them off!'

***

Nash provided what was needed to put Jared's plan to work. Jared had spotted a gang member keeping watch a time or two. They appeared more concerned with him than anyone else. There was a chance they had heard of him. To be safe, he gave Nash's potion to Payne, along with instructions for Tolkin. When he weathered the storm to check on his horses, he was sure someone kept an eye on him. That worked to his advantage, as Payne was able to visit Tolkin without anyone paying attention to him.

126

After chatting with Denny for a few minutes and looking over the horses, Jared made his way over to the coal, tools and lumber yard store. There was a table and several chairs set up next to the stove, where a coffee pot was brewing. Payne had arrived and was already nursing a cup.

'Pour you some?' Joe asked. 'It ain't great, but it's hot and it's free.'

'Thanks,' Jared replied, shrugging out of his coat. 'Not much new snow, but it's still a ground blizzard due to that ferocious wind. And, boy, it cuts through a man like one of those logging saws going through a sapling.'

Payne taunted, 'Yeah, and you ain't much for size. Best keep some rocks in your pockets to keep from getting blowed away.'

'The guns of our bandit gang are the only thing that worries me about getting blown away.'

'You said you had this all planned out,' Joe spoke up, filling a cup with coffee for Jared. 'I only signed on with this scheme because Nash promised it would work.'

'He's the only brother Jared told me about who don't know how to shoot,' Payne quipped. 'And you're taking his word?'

Joe handed Jared the cup and sighed. 'Let's not talk about how many ways this plan can blow up in our face. Which of those men are we gonna take down first? And then, how do we keep the others from knowing about it?'

Jared took a sip of coffee. Joe hadn't exaggerated about the taste, but it was good and hot. His body thanked him for the internal heat, while he ignored the flavour.

Payne drummed his fingers nervously on the table. 'Maybe we ought to do this in a more permanent fashion. You know, slip in and kill them in their sleep a couple at a time.'

'Some men don't sleep that soundly,' Jared dismissed his notion. 'One man cries out or fights back and we'd have the rest of them to deal with. My gun only carries six loads. Which of you is going to stop the other six?'

'Cal said there might be another problem with our guests,' Joe cautioned. 'Ever since they arrived, a few of the gang have remained up all night. Tolkin leaves the saloon at midnight, but Yates told Cal two or three of the jokers don't head for their rooms until daylight.'

'Men on the run are cautious,' Payne spoke to Jared. 'Now, besides keeping a coupla men up nights, they are watching you.'

'They probably suspect we've figured out they are a gang of outlaws. The good thing about their staying alert is the fact it wears them down, and it splits their forces. That should help Tolkin put the first of our plan into action. If we can eliminate the night guards without any of the others being the wiser, we might just make this work.'

'Then we're doing it tonight... blizzard or no,' Joe confirmed.

'The storm could let up at any time. We don't dare wait until fair weather. These boys are getting cabin fever as it is. We have to strike before they decide to disarm us all... or worse.'

CHAPTER ELEVEN

Shane stood next to Chris as they looked out of the general store window. The morning had brought more wind, and gusts that shook the building. The snow blizzards were like great white sheets flapping wildly about on a clothesline – impossible to see through, until crossing the street had become a five-minute test of survival.

'Not much let-up today,' Chris made the comment. 'We'd never have lasted through the night.'

Shane sighed. 'Yeah, and it's too late to think about going anywhere today. I'm beginning to wonder if this blizzard will never blow itself out. I'll bet half of Kranston's herd is dead by now. We had the canyon to protect our beef, with the stacks of hay and the silos to fall back on. Even so, we might lose several hundred head. Can't expect animals to find any food in this endless cold and blowing snow.'

'Going to be the end of a lot of ranches, especially if these blizzards keep coming.'

'Nature's way of compensating for overgrazing and too many cattle. Even the few remaining buffalo will be hard pressed to survive this kind of weather.'

'It's a shame we couldn't get to Castle Point and help Jared,' Chris said. 'A dozen gunmen, in a town with only a few civilians?'

Shane flashed him a confident grin. 'I'd wager Jer is telling Nash there's nothing to worry about. He's probably telling him that more men would just get in his way.'

Chris chuckled, in spite of the grave situation. 'Darcy said you thought of him as a hero.'

He laughed. 'I reckon I do. But the few times we've been in trouble together, Jer always knew what needed to be done. He has a special way of thinking, no matter what the job or odds.'

'Well, taking on a dozen killers, I hope he rounds up a little help. That's a powerful lot of men to keep track of during a gunfight.'

'I still wish we'd have gotten the message right away. By the time the weather clears up, it's sure to be too late.'

'It got down to ten below zero last night. If the sky clears, the temperature will drop another twenty degrees. This is like nothing I've ever seen before, Shane, not even in Montana.'

'No one I've talked to ever saw it this bad. All we can hope for is an early spring.'

'We've still got six to eight weeks of winter ahead,' Chris said, regret thick in his voice. 'I wonder if any of our cattle will survive.'

'Or any of us,' Shane agreed. 'How many people will run out of fuel or food? How many cow hands are going to freeze to death trying to save their herd?'

'Stop staring out the window!' Darcy barked the order from behind the two men. 'The food is on the table, and we don't want anyone talking gloom and doom and devastation over the dinner table. You hear me?'

Chris regarded her with a disarming gaze. 'Your eyes glow like burning embers when you get your dander up, Miss Darcy. Durned if you aren't beautiful no matter what your mood!'

130

Shane laughed, not so much at the remark, but because of the instant flush of colour that came into his sister's cheeks. 'We'll be good, sis,' he promised, trying to soothe her discomfiture. 'No more talking about the end of the world until after the meal.'

She spun about with her shoulders erect and marched off towards the rear of the store where Skip and his wife lived.

'You sure called it, Shane,' Chris whispered. 'Fire and ice!'

***

Elko joined Gauge and Hayworth for their evening meal. Lazelle and two of his men were just leaving the eatery, but none of them gave so much as a nod in his direction.

'The distrust is so strong in this room a man can hardly take a deep breath,' he remarked to the pair. 'What's the special?'

'Stew again,' Hayworth muttered. 'I believe they're running low on supplies.'

'Yeah, twelve extra mouths will do that to a small settlement like this,' Elko granted.

The waiter arrived and he told him to bring the same meal as his friends at the table. As the waiter left, he heaved a weary sigh.

'If these blizzards don't quit, we're all going to go cabin crazy. The longest walk I've taken in the last two days was to the stable and back. The horses are bunched together like they was jammed inside a stock car. They barely step outside to get a breath of air.'

'Even animals know not to go out in weather like this,' Hayworth said. 'I've never seen the like, day after day, one blizzard after another. I'm beginning to wonder if this

131

is going to freeze over the entire country. Are we gonna become one of them ice burgs, like's in the ocean?'

Gauge grunted. 'Who can say? Could be God's wrath. Maybe He is fed up with mankind.'

'Just so long as He isn't aiming His guns only at us!'

'No, Elko,' Hayworth responded to the man's dire concern. 'This storm covers Canada and a dozen states and territories. It's gonna punish man and beast for a thousand miles in all directions. We just happen to be in the middle of it.'

'Well, it's sure enough getting to Lazelle. That man is wound tight as a bobcat in a flour sack,' Elko declared. 'He's got a trapped animal look about him: frantic, edgy, and more than a little unhinged. I wouldn't put it past him to try and take over the town – maybe do away with us at the same time.'

Gauge waved a hand for calm. 'He isn't that crazy.'

'We're all snowbound,' Haywood observed. 'There are people who can't stand confinement. He could be one of them.'

Gauge considered his logic and his mind worked swiftly. 'Who's got the watch tonight?'

'It's their turn,' Hayworth said. Lazelle has Braden and Rogers on the long shift. Webster and Hofman are the other two staying up until midnight.'

'Then we've got our inside man on the overnight watch. That's good. We need to make sure at least one of our men is keeping an eye on things. If Lazelle thinks he can catch us sleeping, we'll shut down that idea right away.'

'So long as Braden doesn't turn against us,' Elko warned. 'If they suspect he is working with us, they might take him out first.'

'We could always move against them before they have the chance,' Hayworth suggested. 'Truth is, Lazelle is the man causing the real threat. The two blacks don't seem eager to be drawn into a fight for leadership, nor does Rogers. As for Vaughn, he's a follower. Norris is his only true ally.'

'And all of them have to know the odds are against a takeover. We've got the three of us who can run our team – Lazelle has only himself. Norris isn't a leader.'

The food arrived and the three of them began to eat.

'Elko,' Gauge instructed between bites, 'you make sure one of our side is on the night watch from now on. We can't be too careful with Laz. This being cooped up is making us all jumpy, but let's not give him an opening to do something stupid.'

'Seems to be his natural state,' Hayworth observed.

'Dangerous and stupid are a bad combination,' Elko chipped back at him.

'Yeah, well, we want to be prepared for whatever action the man might take,' Gauge warned. 'Soon as we get a clear day, we'll strip this town to the bone and head for Laramie. The minute we arrive, we'll find a private spot and split up the shares from the loot. Then everyone can go their own way.'

'I'll look forward to that day,' Hayworth said. 'Yessir, I'm gonna be a happy man when we get to Laramie.'

***

Jared and Payne moved to the window and looked inside the saloon. The ice had glazed over the glass, but the table with the four men was visible.

'Looks like they're out!' Payne said, unable to conceal his excitement. 'Tolkin did the job!'

Jared signalled to Nash. He, Cal and Joe hurried over to where they remained at the window. All three were shivering, but not from the cold. None of these men had never been involved in a daring strategy like this, and their trembling stemmed from nerves and fright.

'Are you ready?' Jared asked them as a group. 'There's no turning back once we start.'

Tolkin opened the door and stuck his head out. 'Hey! We doing this or what?' he called in a hushed voice. 'Time's a wasting!'

Jared and Payne went to the table. Payne picked up the bottle and examined it. 'Drank about half of it,' he said.

'All right then,' Jared stated firmly. 'It looks like the chloral hydrate did the job. Nash, you three and Tolkin get those four bodies over to Denny. He'll need some help securing the prisoners.'

'What about you?' Nash wanted to know.

'Me and Payne will visit the Mexicans in the hotel and try and get them out quietly. If any shooting starts, the plan will be to save your own hides.'

'Great vote of confidence for us,' Cal grumbled.

'Get moving!' Jared ordered.

Yates had come out from the back room to help with the removal of the four men at the card table. All of them were completely unresponsive. Nash grabbed one outlaw under his armpits and Cal took hold of his feet. Tolkin and Joe did the same with a second. As they carted them to the door, Yates held it open for them. As quickly as they could get the first two over to the barn, they would return for the other two. Everything had to move rapidly. If one gang member discovered what was happening, they all risked being killed.

Meanwhile, Jared and Payne hurried next door to the hotel.

'Glad it isn't snowing,' Payne said. 'I can almost see where we're going.'

'Still a bitter cold wind,' Jared replied. 'Keep your gun-hand in your pocket until we get up the stairs. We have to move like ghosts. I'm sure Elko will be a light sleeper.'

'I hear you, Pard. You lead the way and I'll do my best to step lightly.'

They entered the hotel and were met by Judy, the elderly woman who ran the place. She handed Jared a pass key that opened every door and advised them that all men were accounted for.

'The two Mexicans are in the number one room at the top of the stairs she outlined. The second pair – Elko and Hayworth, turned in about an hour ago. They are in room number four. The two men in the single rooms, numbers five and six, have also retired for the night.'

'Thank you, Judy,' Jared said. 'Get yourself to bed and lock your door until this is over. If you hear shooting, stay there until one of us gives you the all clear.'

'May God watch over you and the others,' she said softly. 'Be careful.'

The lady disappeared into her bedroom, which was located behind the counter. Jared led the way to the stairway and stopped. 'Rooms one, two and three are on the left. Two and three are occupied by a family and two salesmen. They've been warned to stay inside and not investigate any noise or gunshots.'

'I'm hoping there won't be any gunshots,' Payne said, not hiding his concern. 'I done warned you I don't shoot for shucks.'

Jared put a finger to his lips for quiet and led the way. Payne stuck right on his heels. Both of them were fully aware that if they messed up with the two Mexicans, it would likely raise the alarm for the other four outlaws upstairs. If shooting started, the men from the rooming house would be alerted too. Against such odds, it was unlikely that either the plan or Jared and Payne would survive.

Stopping at the room marked one, Jared carefully tested the door knob. It was not locked. He tipped a nod to Payne. 'Trusting sorts, this pair. Gotta' love 'em for that.'

Payne pulled his knife, getting ready. Judy had dimmed the two lamps near the downstairs entrance way that were kept on at night. It cut down on how much light would shine into the room when the door opened.

Jared eased the door a crack, then very slowly opened it wide enough to peek inside. With very little light, it was difficult to make out the two beds. However, there was no movement and one of the men was snoring. Payne pressed up next to Jared, ready to enter the room. Jared pulled his hunting knife and whispered softly over his shoulder.

'Pin them to the bed. Make sure your guy doesn't cry out.'

'He ain't gonna say much with me wringing his chicken neck!' Payne assured Jared. 'Ready when you are.'

They moved inside together, each turning to a bed on their side of the room. Jared's man was the one snoring, lying on his back. Jared paused a moment, allowing Payne to get into position. With a quiet 'Now!' he drove a fist into his man's stomach. The breath rushed from his lungs and Jared immediately put the knife blade under his chin and held him down.

'Quiet!' he hissed the threat. 'One peep out of you and I'll separate your head from your body!'

There came a gagging sound from the other bandit. Payne had one knee in the man's middle and a huge paw gripping him around the throat.

'When I remove my hand,' the teamster warned, 'you can take a breath. Anything more than breathing, I'll slit your throat from ear to ear!'

136

Subdued by the unexpected night visitors, the two men offered no resistance. Jared directed them to put on their boots. After checking each man and their coats for weapons, they let them bundle up. When the men were ready to move, Jared bound their hands behind their backs with thin strips of rawhide.

'You both speak good English, right?' he asked the two men.

They both gave an affirmative nod.

'One thump, one heavy step, or kicking the wall or stairs – anything that would wake a sleeping deer – and we kill you both. You understand? Savvy?'

'Si. We understand,' one of the duo replied.

The four of them left the room and made a careful, silent descent down the stairs. Once out into the night, Jared hurried them along the snowy path to the barn. Denny and the others were finishing up with the four men from the saloon.

Jared turned the Mexicans over to Denny and stopped to watch the blacksmith's handiwork.

He had several three-foot lengths of chain with a single shackle at one end. At the opposite end of the chain, he had attached a large ring. A couple taps with his hammer set a rivet that secured the shackle around the outlaw's wrist. When each had a cuff in place, the two men were put inside the special wagon. It still looked like a prairie schooner, but there had been some additions. Denny explained to Nash and the others as he directed the two men to sit, one on either side of the wagon.

'Double wall to protect the driver,' Denny began. 'The outlaws sit with one arm next to the sidewall of the wagon, with the chain hanging over the side. The rails running from the sideboards and going overhead for the canopy have been reinforced. In essence, they are like the steel bars on a prison wagon. When the chain on their wrists is dangling over the side of the wagon, the ring at the other end of their shackle is threaded through by a second chain. It runs along the sideboards from front to back.'

He moved around and took the ring from the man on that side. 'You see? I take this chain from where it's anchored at the front, run it through the ring, then attach it to the back of the wagon. It holds all six prisoners on this side so they can't get out of the wagon. I do the same on the other side with the other six. And there you be – as sound a prison wagon as the one they send from Cheyenne.'

Cal marvelled at the set-up. 'It gives the man both hands to eat with or keep their blankets in place, yet they can't move more than a couple of feet. What a great idea!'

'Wa'al, it does mean they have to sleep leaning together.' Denny laughed. 'Then again, they's all good friends, all members of the same gang of cut-throats. I'm sure they'll get along just fine.'

'OK,' Jared said. 'We're half way there. You fellows stand by and keep guard here. Me and Payne will go round up the others.'

'Your plan is working like a brand-new timepiece,' Nash praised their success. 'Let's hope nothing goes wrong with the second half.'

***

Norris had felt queasy ever since dinner. He had left early from the table and went to bed. When the churning rousted him from sleep, he observed Vaughn had come to bed. He quietly put on his boots and coat and headed for the saloon. Sometimes a beer would help calm his irritable stomach. If the two extra men had turned in for the night, he would sit in on a game with Rogers and Braden. It was their turn for the long shift.

He wrapped his arms around himself, hurrying down the walkway, ducking against the bite of the ever-present wind. He was relieved it wasn't snowing. Maybe they would actually get a couple good days so they could head for Laramie. He was sick to death of this nothing settlement. No real gambling house, no women, nothing to do but sit. If he ever…

Norris glanced though the pane of the saloon's front window and skidded to a halt. The table was empty!

'What the hell?' he gasped. He pressed against the glass and looked at the clock on the wall above the bar. It read half-past eleven 'o clock. All four men should have still been playing cards.

His heart began to pound and his breath was suddenly short. What could have happened? Why would all of the men be missing? It's as if….

Wait a minute! He paused in thought.

All four men worked for Lazelle. Did that mean something? It's true, Braden got along well with both gangs, but this? It made no sense. Why would those men desert their post? Lazelle would have their heads for not doing the job given them. Was it possible that Gauge or Laz had ordered them to do a special chore? But what kind of chore would they be doing in the middle of the night?

Norris reversed his direction and started for the rooming house. No, he decided, stopping in his tracks. If something was going on, there would be activity at the hotel. As he approached the building, he wondered if this might be a move by Gauge to eliminate Lazelle and his men. If so, there should be men moving about, perhaps even a couple of his friends being held prisoner.

But slipping into the hotel told him nothing. It was completely quiet. No one was stirring; nothing appeared to be going on at all. Norris swore under his breath and left the building. His stomach was roiling, made worse by the mystery of the missing guards. He had to visit the outhouse before doing a more thorough search.

Entering the small hut, he leaned over and heaved. The retching was nasty, but it did help calm his stomach. Taking a few breaths, he decided to check with Vaughn before waking anyone about the missing men. He didn't dare wake up Lazelle without having a very good reason. If Vaughn agreed the missing card players were something to worry about, the two of them would go together and wake up their volatile leader.

CHAPTER TWELVE

Jared and Payne went to the rooming house next. As all four of the men from the card game had been accommodated there, they only had to worry about taking the other two. It should have been a cinch… except when they burst into the room, there was only one man in bed!

Rousing the man, whose name was Vaughn, Payne put a knife to his throat and barked the question: 'Where's your partner? You best tell us right this second or I'll slit your throat!'

Vaughn's eyes bugged with fear, but he shook his head. 'I-I ain't got no idea!' he stammered. 'Norris was sacked out when I come to bed. Honest! I don't know when or where he went.'

Payne studied Jared. 'Do we wait for him?'

'Better to move as quick as possible. With this one tucked away, it only leaves five. If we wait, the other gent could warn the others.'

'Grab your boots and throw on your coat, fella,' Payne ordered. 'Be damn quick about it, or we'll leave your corpse here for your rooming partner to find!'

Keeping a close watch for anyone moving on the streets, Jared led the way back to the barn. Missing one of the men from the rooming house, he was thinking they shouldn't have woken him up. It would have been better to have both men in the room, rather than have one awake and wondering where his friend was at.

'Probably visiting the outhouse,' Payne said, as they neared the stables. 'I should have waited in the room.'

'The fellow might have discovered the missing men at the saloon,' Jared reasoned. 'If that turns out to be the case, we would have been separated, and maybe ended up taking on seven gunmen.'

'He's bound to raise the alarm when he gets back and discovers his bunk mate is missing.'

'Soon as we get this one settled, we'll make a careful approach at the hotel. If we can't sneak up on them, we'll try to pin them upstairs. With them trapped down the right hallway, they'll have no way out. The others can give us a hand to round up the missing man.'

'It might work. The only exit is down the stairs. They expose themselves and we'll shoot them dead. We keep them pinned down until we starve them out or they surrender.'

'It's about the only way we can handle four or five of them.'

'I'll stick with you, in case the shooting starts,' Payne said. 'Your brother, Nash, can slip over and grab my rifle and ammo from our room.'

***

Norris felt a little better, after emptying his stomach. He huddled against the cold wind and started back to his room. He must have missed something when he left the café early. Vaughn and the others might have discussed a job or chore without him. That made sense. Vaughn hadn't wished to wake him, knowing he was feeling ill. So there might be a good reason for the men not being in the saloon. The sky was clear, so it's possible they were readying the horses for travel. Maybe they were going to pull out no matter what the weather.

After entering the rooming house Norris walked to his sleeping quarters. He pushed open the door to his room and stared agape.

'Vaughn?' he stared in surprise at the empty bunk. 'Now, where the hell did you go?'

He quickly inspected the room. No tussle, nothing amiss, only Vaughn's boots, coat and hat were missing. Disturbingly, he hadn't taken his rifle or gunbelt.

Norris stood rigid, numb from shock and totally confused. Vaughn might have gone to the hotel. Maybe he woke up and wondered where his roommate was. He could have joined the four men from the saloon for a special reason, but that made no sense. If some action had been planned, surely Vaughn would have woke him or tried to find him. No, this mystery didn't feel like a good thing. He had to find out what was going on.

Checking his pistol, Norris decided he had no options. He left the rooming house and returned to the hotel. Hurrying up the stairs, he decided to first check on the Mexicans. If they were in their room, there might be a simple explanation for the missing men.

Knowing they never locked their door, he quietly pushed it open to take a peek inside. A cold shiver ran through his entire body.

'Fer the love of…' They were gone too!

Spinning about, he swept the hotel lobby with his eyes. Nothing.

Where could these two have gone? His mind was reeling as he went down the second hallway. He paused to carefully test the doorknob to Hayworth and Elko's room.

It was secure. He placed his ear to the door. The sound of heavy breathing reached his ears. Moving quickly to Gauge's door, he could also make out he was in bed.

Moving over to Lazelle's door, he had to knock three times before he got an answer.

Lazelle had sleep in his eyes and a sour expression on his face when he yanked the door open.

'Norris! You'd better have a good excuse for waking me.'

Norris strode forwards, physically pushing the man back inside the room. He turned quickly to close the door. 'One question, boss,' he said to the stunned man. 'Do you have something going on with the men tonight? Did you issue some special orders while I was sick in bed?'

Lazelle ran his hand over his nearly bald head and made a face. 'What the Sam Hill are you yammering about, Norris? Make sense!'

'The men in the saloon are missing,' he reported.

'Say what?'

'They're gone,' Norris told him. 'I was going to have a beer with them, but all four of them are missing. I went back to my room to check with Vaughn, and he's gone too. I wasn't away from the room for fifteen minutes and he's plum disappeared!'

The boss man was wide awake now. Fear, anger, confusion… it all mixed together until ire took control. Then he walked over and grabbed his gun. As he was strapping the belt around his waist, he began to sort out the situation.

'What does it all mean, Norris?'

'Dunno, boss. Near as I could tell, Gauge, Elko and Hayworth are in their rooms. The thing is, the Mexicans are not in their room.'

'It was our turn to keep watch over the town,' he said, his mind working hard to make sense of what Norris was telling him.

'I think Gauge is making a move against us,' Norris voiced his opinion. 'He must have overheard us planning a doublecross. Could be, Braden let the news slip... maybe on purpose.'

'What? Why would he sell us out?'

'I seen him and Gauge talking a couple days back. They didn't know anyone was watching, and it was only the two of them. I couldn't hear what was being said, but there was a lot of head-bobbin' going on.'

'If that's so, then the Mexicans took our boys somewhere and locked them up. It's the only thing that makes sense... unless the town folks have taken up arms against us?'

'Fat chance of that,' Norris stated with disdain. 'Most of these storekeeps and clerks don't wear a gun. They are a bunch of family men, with kids. We've been keeping a close eye on them all, and aside from the doctor's brother, there ain't a man in town that looks capable with a gun. It has to be Gauge.'

Lazelle was seething, struggling to control his rage. 'I can't believe the man managed something like this. But Vaughn and you... you were the only ones not at the saloon.' He swore vehemently and punched a fist into his other palm. 'It's a takeover for sure! Gauge learned what we had in mind about taking all the loot for ourselves. He's moved first and grabbed our men. Gauge is the one running the show!'

'Damn, boss!' Norris exclaimed 'We're in major trouble! That means there are only the two of us left.'

'They must be saving me for last.'

'They'll be coming for you any minute,' Norris warned. 'With me in the wind, they'll know I've come to warn you.'

'We've got to hit them right now, before they're ready.'

'What's your thinking?' Norris wanted to know.

'They must have a couple guys watching the men they've grabbed – probably the Mexicans, and maybe Braden, too.

145

I'll bet Gauge is sleeping like a babe, him figuring he'll take me by myself in the morning.'

'My being on the loose might change that.'

'That's why we hit them now, before they figure out where you went. The two of us will take care of the three of them, then we'll track down the Mexicans and free the rest of our boys.'

***

As Jared and Payne took up a position near the hotel, Nash came out of the darkness with the teamster's rifle. He had a small bag with his extra bullets.

'Took some digging,' Nash told Payne, 'but here are all of the rounds I could find.'

'Ought to be enough,' Jared said. 'If this turns into a standoff, we'll round up all of the ammo and guns we left at the rooming house. No way will they get down the stairs with us having them…'

But gunfire erupted!

'Stay out of the line of fire, Nash!' Jared yelled at his brother, while reaching for the door handle. 'Come on, Payne. Stay low and keep to cover.'

Elko, hearing Norris knocking to wake Lazelle, had been curious enough to get out of bed. He alerted Hayworth and opened the door. He had his gun in hand when the two men came charging out of the room. Before he could inquire as to what was going on, both men turned guns on him.

Lazelle and Norris pulled their triggers at the same time. Elko was hit by both rounds, but managed to get off a shot of his own, nailing Norris squarely in the chest. He staggered backwards into Hayworth. The ex-army sergeant wrapped an arm around him to hold him up and returned fire at both men.

146

From the downstairs, Jared saw the muzzle flashes and pushed Payne behind a wall for cover. Gauge entered the mix as guns continued to blast from three doorways in the hall. One of his bullets found its mark, striking Lazelle in the ribs. Lazelle put another round in the already wounded Elko, but Hayworth got off a well-aimed shot that struck the bald man in the head. He dropped like a sack of flour, landing partially on top of Norris.

Gauge cautiously left his room as Norris and Lazelle were both down. He kept his gun pointed at the two wounded and dying men, while hurrying over to his two men. Hayworth had been holding Elko up, but allowed his body to sag to the floor.

Jared and Payne slowly approached up the stairs, guns ready for use. 'What's going on?' Jared called to the two men. 'What's all the shooting about?'

Gauge was on his knees. He lifted Elko's head up with a gentle hand, saddened by the death of his best friend. Hayworth cast a sharp look at Jared, but didn't turn his gun on him. Both men seemed in a confused daze.

Jared holstered his weapon, seeing there was no fight left in the two survivors. He discovered Nash had followed after them.

'The shooting stopped,' Nash explained his approach to Jared. 'Let me have a look. Maybe I can help one of the wounded.'

But Jared shook his head. 'All three of them look to be dead,' he replied.

'How about you two?' Payne spoke to Gauge and Hayworth. 'Either of you get hit?'

'I'm fine,' Hayworth said. 'Elko was in front of me. He took every round.'

Gauge lowered his friend to the floor and sat back on his heels. 'Same here. Laz got off a shot at me, but he missed.'

'What caused the gunfight?' Jared asked Gauge.

'Laz has been wanting to take over the gang. I guess he decided the time had come.' He shrugged. 'Makes no sense, just the two of them trying to kill us.' He frowned, looking down the hallway. 'Where the hell are the Mexicans? Did they kill them in their sleep?'

'Actually,' Jared informed him, taking on a lawman's stance, 'we have all of the others in custody.' At the shocked looks on Hayworth and Gauge's faces, he added professionally: 'You're both under arrest.'

***

Once the two remaining outlaws were locked in place with the others, the bodies of the three dead men were wrapped in blankets and put in a storage shed. When the army arrived, they could take the bodies back with them, along with the prisoners. With the chore finished, all of the men returned home to their beds, with the exception of Jared, Payne and Denny. They were determining the best method for keeping watch over the nine prisoners.

Gauge admitted that Elko had cut the telegraph wires about a mile down the line, both of those going to Cheyenne, and the one going westwards. Jared announced to Payne and Denny that he would use snowshoes, if need be, and find the breaks as soon as it was light.

'In that case,' Payne offered. 'I'll keep watch over the prisoners tonight. You can relieve me long enough for breakfast in the morning, then get to repairing those lines. We don't want to keep watch over these varmints any longer than necessary.'

'I'll go along with that,' Denny said. 'I ain't got room to turn around, what with the wagon and all these extra horses. It's costing me a fortune in coal to keep both the stove and the forge going twenty-four hours a day.'

Jared yawned. 'All right. It seems we have a plan in mind for the time being. Both Payne and I will take turns helping watch the outlaws tomorrow.'

'We need to gather up the money they stole and have it ready to turn over to the army,' Payne pointed out.

'Nash and Cal can handle that end of things.'

Denny said: 'And we're gonna need extra help to feed and watch over these critters at nights.'

'We'll get more help and make a schedule for covering shifts until the army can get here,' Jared directed. 'With those irons you made in place, there's no way our guests are going to get loose. It will be nothing more than a waiting game, once I get the telegraph working.'

'Let's have us a victory drink and call it a night,' Payne offered. He produced a bottle of whiskey from his coat. 'Grab a couple tin-cups or we can just pass the jug around. I'm figuring we all deserve a toast for this night's work.'

Denny rounded up three cups and Payne poured three-fingers worth in each. The he capped the bottle and tucked it back in his coat. The trio touched the tins together and downed the few swallows as one.

'OK,' Payne announced. 'I got this here watch for the rest of the night. Sounds like the wind is gonna howl, so you two best try and catch a few winks before daylight.'

Denny snorted. 'Ain't gonna see daylight till noon from the sound of it.'

Jared bid the two goodnight and turned up his collar to make the walk back to the clinic. It was beginning to snow, and had it not been for the light of a lamp showing, he would have had to feel his way to reach Nash's place. Trina and Nash were still up.

'They have a term: paranoia,' Nash spoke up as Jared shrugged out of his coat. 'It's a sense of thinking people are after you. In a gang like the one we've been dealing with, they had two leaders and neither trusted the other. If it hadn't been for the winter weather forcing them to stay together, they would have likely split up shortly after the robbery. The mistrust grew until it finally split the gang.'

Jared laughed. 'Yeah, we thought we might have to shoot a couple of them if they put up a fight, but they were too busy fighting one another to even suspect we would take action against them. I never seen such a shocked look on a man's face as when I told Gauge he was under arrest.'

'Can I get you anything?' Trina asked.

'The only thing I need is sleep,' Jared replied. 'I can hardly keep my eyes open.'

'Then head for your room,' Nash instructed. 'I'll get the lamps and we'll turn in. It's been a long night for all of us.'

CHAPTER THIRTEEN

Jared felt someone shaking him, but his brain was on a blissful vacation. He was warm and comfortable, which made coming full awake downright unpleasant.

'Jerry!' Nash's words broke through the heavy fog. 'Wake up! Come on, big brother! We've got trouble!'

The alarm in Nash's voice shocked his system to consciousness. Jared sat up, but he remained oddly disoriented and only vaguely aware of his surroundings.

'I'm up,' he mumbled, though he still couldn't get his brain to function properly.

'Here!' Nash put a cup to his lips. 'Take a couple sips of this.'

Jared took a gulp and his eyes popped open wide. He coughed and shook his head. 'Dad-gum, Nash! What did you put in my cup – turpentine?'

'A mixture of alcohol and Cayenne pepper!'

'Gimme a drink of water!' Jared cried. 'The inside of my mouth is on fire.'

Trina arrived with a full cup of soothing water and handed it to him. 'I told you that you were using too much pepper,' she scolded her husband.

Jared took the first swallow, then sloshed a second around in his mouth. After doing the same two or three

151

times, he could finally breathe normally. To Nash's credit the potion worked. The fog abated and Jared could think rationally.

'You said there was trouble? Did the prisoners escape?'

Nash harrumphed. 'They're gone, but they didn't escape.'

Jared stared at him, totally perplexed. 'Maybe my brain isn't as clear as I thought. Trot that by me a second time.'

'Show him what you found,' Trina prompted.

'In a minute, darling. I want to be sure Jer is...'

Jared reached out and grabbed Nash by the front of his jacket. 'Tell me!' he flared hotly. 'What has happened?'

'First off, you were drugged – both you and Denny. I believe Payne used the same bottle Tolkin prepared for the gang playing poker.'

'O... K,' Jared allowed, slowly absorbing the information. 'It makes no sense whatsoever, but I understand that much. I've never had a sleep like this before. What else?'

'Payne hitched up his team and took the prison wagon.'

Jared scowled. 'Took it...Where did he take it?'

'No way to tell,' his brother reported. 'The wind is blowing something fierce. The tracks were already wiped clean and buried by the time Cal came to tell me what had happened. It's hard to see the buildings across the street; I can't imagine why your pal took off in a storm like this.'

'The money! What about...'

Nash gave his head a negative toss. 'No, I've got the money right here in the house. Me and Cal did a clean sweep of the rooms being used by the gang members. We've recovered most of the army payroll and that from the bank too. The two leaders kept the money in their rooms.'

Jared rubbed his eyes to remove the last of the sleep, then stared off into space. 'He can't possibly make it to

Cheyenne, not with so much snow – and in a confounded blizzard! I'll bet his horses don't last but four or five miles. That wagon probably weighs a ton or more, carrying nine men in the back, combined with all that special fortification Denny added.'

'Show him the box,' Trina urged her husband a second time.

'What box? What are you talking about?'

Nash held out a cigar box. 'I was searching for extra ammo when I found it. I thought it might hold some bullets.'

Jared took the box, then paused to look at the faces of his brother and sister-in-law. Their expressions were dire, tragic even. A feeling of foreboding filled the room and imbued Jared to his very soul. There could be nothing but misery inside the cigar box.

'It's locks of hair,' Trina murmured, her voice like a whisper of death. 'Several different colours.'

Jared lifted the lid and grimaced. '*The killer takes a hank of his victim's hair,*' were the words US Deputy Marshal John Reinhold had said. They knew of four women, but there were five locks – one that looked like it actually had some grey in it.

'My dear Lord,' Jared murmured in a reverent tone of voice. 'Payne is the woman killer. He's the man I was searching for.'

Nash wondered, 'You think he discovered I had mistakenly found and opened his trophy box?'

'He gave us the drink before even returning to his room.'

Trina shook her head. 'He never came back to his room. I never slept a wink all night; I would have heard him.'

Jared ducked his head to hide the tears that burned at the back of his eyes. 'We discussed the shortage of supplies

153

here in town, and how a dozen extra mouths to feed might put everyone in a bind. All of those men were facing a noose, due to the men they killed during their robberies, plus the two old-timers who ran a little trading post some twenty miles from here.'

'But to take them out in this blizzard,' Nash was grave. 'It'll mean the death of them all, and that includes Payne.'

'He's taking the easy way out,' Jared determined. 'He didn't want to face a judge and jury for killing those women, women who were in the same profession as his mother. I believe his conscience finally got the better of him.'

'What now?' Nash wanted to know. 'There's no way to know which way he went. The trails out of town go in every direction.'

'My first order of business will be to reconnect the telegraph lines. Then, if the weather clears, I'll start looking for the wagon.'

'The wind is gusting thirty or forty miles an hour, Jerry. You'll be lucky to find the telegraph poles, let alone figure out which way Payne went.'

'My first priority is to get the telegraph working,' he voiced his resolve. 'I can keep the line in sight until I locate the break. I have to get a message to Valeron and stop the family from trying to send help. We don't want any of our people to die out there in this storm, especially now the danger is past.'

Nash agreed. 'Trina has the makings for breakfast, then we'll pack you a meal to take with you. Just make sure you take the fixings to mend the line. Hate to see you make the trip to the break and not be able to repair it.'

154

***

Payne felt frozen to the seat of the wagon. He had given the bottle of whiskey – laced with chloral hydrate – to the prisoners. The original four hadn't stirred at all, and the others hadn't made a peep in the last four hours. Taking a random trail out of town, he had no idea where he was, only that he had travelled a solid five or six miles.

His team ploughed through the snowdrifts until late afternoon, when they no longer had the strength to pull the wagon any further. When they finally stopped, he climbed down from the wagon seat and waded out to remove their harness. It was no easy chore, with frozen fingers and the wind and crystals of ice nearly taking the skin off his face. Once the animals were free, he turned them back towards town and swatted them on the rumps to get them started. Having been safe, warm and fed in the barn, they would return home to it.

Staggering against the storm's fury, he waded to the back of the wagon. All nine men were unconscious, due to drinking the whiskey. Perhaps they deserved a more fitting punishment, like being hanged, but feeding them took food out of the mouths of the people in Castle Point. He climbed into the rear opening and located the bottle. It had about two or three swallows left.

'Much obliged, fellow criminals,' he told the sleeping group. 'I reckon I'll join you. Looks downright cozy in here, all of you hunkered down and resting.' Sitting down, the notion that this was the last thing he would do in his lifetime crept into his mind. He thought of Jared Valeron, a friend he had made, a friend who would be devastated when he learned the truth. If only he had met someone like him when he was younger, before making the mistake of visiting his mother.

The memory still made him sick inside. At the age of twenty-five she hadn't even recognized him. When he had tried to talk to her, she had tugged on his arm and tried to lead him to her bed. She was drunk and crass, asking how much money he would pay to lie with her.

Payne swallowed a hard lump that tried to rise in his throat. He visualized the shocked look on her face, when he told her who he was… as he wrung the last breath from her lungs.

Women ought to be forced to get a licence before having children, he thought. His mother lamented endlessly how he had ruined her life. Well, she hadn't done him any favours, either. Ducking his head, he felt ashamed and full of regret for having killed those other women. They hadn't done a thing to deserve being strangled. They'd been innocent victims, the same as he had been. He wished he knew how to pray, but he doubted even a benevolent god would forgive his wickedness.

He lifted his head, tipped the bottle to his lips and said: 'Here's to you, Jared. I hope you can forgive me for what I done.'

Payne took the last swallows of his life and leaned back against the railing, awaiting sleep… and an icy death.

**

It was near bedtime and well below zero when a youngster brought word to the clinic that Payne's prize team of horses had returned to the barn. Throwing on his coat, Jared made the short trip to the livery. He discovered Denny had just stoked the fire.

'Wind and snow let up about dark,' the blacksmith informed Jared, leading him over to the animals. 'The four mares come plodding in a little bit ago, looking to be on

156

their last legs. I just finished giving all of them a good rub-down. And I've added a little whiskey to their oats. I think they'll be fine.'

Jared said: 'I managed to get the telegraph line back up and working, but the blowing snow made it impossible to search for the prison wagon. If I hadn't had the poles to follow, I'd never have made it back to town.'

'For sure, old man winter has been tossing a real fit today. I never left the barn until the snow finally let up. Whilst I was having a meal at the café, Cal told me you got back in one piece. It's why I sent the town runner to let you know about the horses.'

'Come morning, I'll take a horse and see if I can follow the trail left by the team. As cold as it is, and having turned loose his team, I don't expect to find Payne or any of the others alive. We'll have to store the bodies until the army arrives.'

'Gotta wonder why Payne took off like he done. He seemed a genuinely nice fella.'

'He was,' Jared said. 'Like most people, he had his faults. I'll miss him, but I understand why he sacrificed himself to be rid of that gang of outlaws.'

'His actions might save the lives of a few people here-abouts. If the roads stay socked in, we might not get another delivery of goods for a month or more. Be tough to keep from starving as it is, without them extra mouths to feed.'

'I sent a wire off to Valeron,' Jared turned to other busi-ness. 'Skip – the telegrapher – answered back. Several men did make an attempt to get here, but the blizzard was too much for them. It's a good thing we didn't need them.'

'We done OK on our own, thanks to you and the team-ster. The plan you thought up worked real good.'

Jared grinned. 'It was helped by the two leaders turning on each other.'

'Yes sir,' Denny concurred. 'Otherwise you and Payne might have had a murderous gunfight on your hands.'

'The Lord was watching over us. Everything worked out for the best.'

***

The blizzards continued into February, and the arctic cold dropped temperatures to thirty and even forty below. Relief didn't come until March, when warm Chinook winds began to thaw out the land. The loss of cattle throughout the country was devastating. With the resumption of stagecoach travel again, the newspapers touted stories of many ranch bankruptcies and the loss of tens of thousands of cattle.

Chris was seated in a chair across from Temple Valeron reading some of the tragic stories when Darcy entered the room.

'You have an oddly satisfied look on your face, Christopher,' she remarked. 'Why is that, when the news is all bad?'

He smiled a greeting and replied, 'It is bad about the many losses, but there is one ray of light.' He clarified, 'There's a story about the McMasters ranch losing almost ninety per cent of their entire herd. He's the cattle baron who drove us off our range up in Montana. I'm sorry about the cattle, but not about him getting his just rewards. He is broke.'

'Do you know how petty your enjoyment over his failure sounds?'

He chuckled. 'See? I've a dark side to me, one that seeks poetic justice.'

She giggled. 'Father and Locke have been rather chipper too, considering the situation.'

'We only lost about a hundred head,' Temple entered the conversation. 'And Reese tells me you lost a meager seven head. Amazing cattle, those Herefords.'

'Yes,' Chris agreed. 'And I have to say, your brother was not exactly shedding tears when he gave me the news that the Kranston Continental Consortium announced their bankruptcy.'

'We shouldn't be needing that range back. We're going to keep the herd size down, at least until the price of beef goes up.'

'With so many cattle lost in what the papers are calling "The Big Die-up", that shouldn't be long in coming.'

Darcy tapped her foot impatiently. 'I'm going to be late for work if we don't get a move on, Christopher.'

'Right you are, my lovely nymph,' he said with a smirk. 'I'll get you to work on time, but once we get our house built, you'll have a job right here on the ranch.'

'Have you a wedding date in mind yet, daughter?' Temple asked.

'I won't even consider a date until Christopher has our house built. I refuse to move into a one-room hut.'

Temple looked at Chris. He had stood up to leave, but winked at him. 'We'll start building as soon as the ground dries up. With everyone pitching in, and working ten to twelve hours a day, it ought to be ready for use by early June.'

'Gwen and I were married on the second of June,' Temple said, a twinkle dancing in his eyes.

'That sounds like a good target date to me.'

'It won't sound near as good if you don't get me to town. If you stand here another minute, I'm going by myself!'

Chris hurried over and opened the front door for her. 'At your service, my lady fair,' he said, bowing gallantly.

'Yes,' Darcy hit him with one of her pixie simpers. 'And that's as it should be.'

'Only till death do us part,' he retorted. 'After that, we are on equal footing.'

She laughed as they went out of the door together. The terrible winter kill had taken its toll on both men and animals. But winter was behind them, spring was in the air, and so too was the love of life and of one another.